KU-153-899

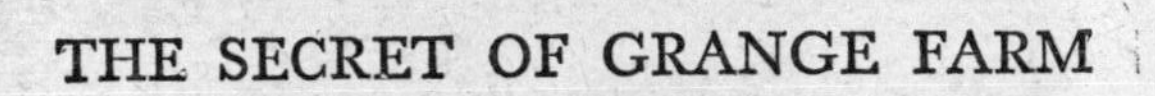
THE SECRET OF GRANGE FARM

THE SECRET OF GRANGE FARM

by

FRANCES COWEN

THE CHILDREN'S PRESS
LONDON AND GLASGOW

PRINTED IN GREAT BRITAIN

CONTENTS

CHAPTER ONE

CHANGE OF PLAN

THE letter from Mavis came by the morning post. Bette carried it up to her room to read before breakfast, which, in her aunt's flat, was taken at eight-thirty. She read it in consternation. It was long and full of rather incoherent apologies, but the gist of it was that Mavis's young sister had contracted measles and Bette could not go and stay with her as they had arranged a couple of weeks ago when term ended.

"Well," said Bette aloud, pushing back her short fair hair, "that is that. So what now!"

In a corner of the room stood two suitcases, one closed, the other opened to receive last-minute things, for she had been actually starting to-morrow for her friend's house in Devon. Everything had been arranged and her aunt, with whom she was now staying, was going up to Scotland to join her husband at the end of the week. This town flat would be closed, and what was she, Bette, to do?

She sat on the edge of the bed, her usually bright face troubled. It was just too bad of Mummy! Getting married like that so suddenly without even discussing it with her, going off to the South of France with her new husband and leaving her, Bette, to the care of relations and friends for the long holidays.

Bette scowled. From the first she had tried to conquer

the jealousy which had assailed her when she had heard the news, but it was with her yet, and, for the moment, she didn't even fight it.

It had been almost the last week of term when she had received the letter from her mother with the astonishing news. Mummy was marrying again, marrying a man Bette did not even know! It was inexplicable, and to Bette it was appalling. From the first she had hated the unknown Mr. Barton Smith with a bitter hatred.

Of course she had told Mavis all about it.

"I can't understand Mummy wanting to marry again. We've been such friends, like sisters almost. After all, my father died long before I was old enough to remember him."

Mavis had surprised her by siding with her mother, whom she knew and liked.

"If he's nice I don't see why not. After all, your mother isn't so very old, thirty-something I'd say, and it must have been lonely for her when you were at school."

"Lonely, with all her friends, and Auntie Joan, and her work?"

Mavis nodded wisely. "And her work! I know she was successful as a dress designer on that magazine, but perhaps she's got tired of working, and well, she met this man and she liked him, I suppose."

"John Barton Smith," Bette had almost sneered, "a lawyer too." Mavis had laughed. "What's wrong with that? He might be very nice."

Impossible to tell Mavis, who, she decided, had failed her, that the very word "lawyer" conjured up a picture of some dry and serious, grey-haired, neat-faced elderly man, sitting in a dusty office. For Bette had only met one lawyer, Mr. Snell, who had charge of her mother's affairs, and she inevitably thought of Mr. Snell.

"After all," Mavis had gone on, "your mother has lived for you these sixteen years, and now she wants a life of her own and a companion who isn't twenty years younger. Why not face it?"

The words had stung, and for the last few weeks she had definitely tried to fight and kill the demon of jealousy which held her. She had made it up with Mavis and gratefully accepted her invitation to come and stay with her during the holidays.

Her mother's wedding, a very quiet one, had coincided with her own sitting for the School Certificate, so she had not even been present. Privately she had been grateful for the excuse; she preferred long hours in the examination hall doing her papers to a rush up to London, meeting "that man", and waving her mother good-bye as she went off on her honeymoon with a stranger. Now Mother, in the South of France, would not be back until the end of August! What a time to go to the South of France! Bette herself had come up to London to stay with Aunt Joan until she joined Mavis, and now, to crown all, this!

What would Aunt Joan think? "I'm in the way," decided Bette miserably, "she won't want to take me up to Scotland with her. What am I to do?"

To whom could she go? She suddenly thought of Nicholas. What made her think of Nicholas Ferndale, her cousin, whom she had not seen for years, she did not know, but her happiest hours as a child had been spent on the old farm in Sussex where Nicholas now stayed after having been abroad. He would have her, of course.

She had been only a child when she had seen him last and he had been in his late teens, but he had taken her everywhere with him, taught her to ride his pony, let her help with the haymaking and taught her innumerable things about birds and the little furtive animals that haunt the hedgerows and woods. This had all been spoiled when he joined the army and was sent to the Far East. Later, in Cyprus, he had been reported missing, and the news that he had been found wounded but alive had come as a wonderful relief to Bette, for she was very fond of her tall, dark-eyed cousin.

Nicky! She would go to him. It was harvest-time too and she would be able to help him on the farm. Then she remembered that her mother had been disappointed in him when she had mentioned him at Christmas. He had only sent them a card, and his letter in answer to hers had been rather trite; a short typed letter saying that he was glad Bette was getting on so nicely at school and that he was busy getting the farm to rights. It had been rather a dull letter in answer to hers, so full of the family news.

"He's been through a great deal," her mother had said. "Now that his father has died and he has been left with that big farm on his hands, I expect he has a lot to do. I wonder how Hugh and Clover are getting on—the farm was always their home too."

Oddly enough Bette could not remember her other cousins so well, but their Uncle Edward, Nicholas's father, had given them a home when their own parents had been killed in a car crash. No, all Bette's attention had been for Nicholas who had entertained and spoiled her.

Bette got up as her aunt called her into breakfast. She decided not to say anything about Mavis's letter; instead she would write to Nicky and invite herself over to Grange Farm on the clear understanding that she would help him with the harvest.

Aunt Joan looked pleased and excited in anticipation of her own holiday. "You've done most of your packing, dear?"

"Everything but last-minute things. I want to buy some sandals though."

"Good. We'll have lunch out to-day and do some last-minute shopping, then we'll go to a film in the afternoon."

Bette agreed with every show of enthusiasm. Now that she had made up her mind, she felt quite pleased with her idea. It would be fun seeing the old Grange Farm again, seeing Nicky, helping him—even better fun than staying with Mavis in her home on the verge of the Devon moors.

Before they went out she went to her room and wrote a hurried letter to her cousin.

"I know it's ages since you saw me and then I was only a child but now I'm quite hefty and will put all I can into helping on the farm." She went on to explain her predicament as shortly as possible, signed it, scrawled the address on the envelope and posted it in the West End that morning.

Looking at Aunt Joan, blissfully ignorant of her change of plan, she was almost persuaded to tell her, but she decided against it. Aunt Joan might insist on waiting for a reply, putting off her journey, and she looked so happy in anticipation of her own holiday that Bette had not the heart to worry her.

Next morning her aunt had to start for Euston early. Bette had formerly planned to take the Torbay express from Paddington at ten-thirty, consequently she remained at the flat to wait for a taxi which would call for her later. When it did come, Bette locked up and left the key with the porter, but instead of going to Paddington she directed the driver to take her to Waterloo.

Brief inquiries elicited that a train to Fairham, the nearest stop to Risely, where Grange Farm was situated, left at eleven-fifteen. Bette whiled away her time in the refreshment room, then caught her train, feeling well pleased with herself.

Had she remained at the flat another hour she might not have felt so happy. A wire arrived for her. The porter took it in and, according to instructions, sent it on to "Care of Mrs. Bentley, Twelve Trees, Forsyth, Scotland".

The wire was brief and to the point.

"*Regret impossible to receive you, writing—Nicholas Ferndale.*"

Fairham is a little, old-fashioned town, much frequented by visitors in the summer. As it is barely ten miles from the coast, people in search of a quiet holiday stay there, motoring or even hiking to the sea when they feel like it.

In the old days when she and her mother had arrived there they had been met by Uncle Edward in a car. Now, as she got off the train she suddenly felt at a loss. Supposing after all Nicky did not want her, suppose he had not even got her letter!

She stood by her two cases, a tall girl, her soft fair hair blowing round her face.

Then someone approached her—a tall fair boy with freckles on his rugged weather-beaten face.

He smiled a trifle diffidently. "I suppose you wouldn't be waiting for someone of the name of Ferndale?"

She brightened at once. "Yes, and you've been sent to meet me. I'm so glad. I was beginning to think that I shouldn't have come after all."

"Not a bit, we're jolly glad to have you. Those your bags? Good, come on then!"

He picked up her cases and led the way to a taxi in the station yard. He spoke to the driver, then got in by her side. Bette smiled at him. "I'm so glad you could have me. I'm going to do my best and help, you know. It's your busiest time, isn't it?"

"Rather, at least we're hoping so," he said oddly, "believe me I never knew what a lot my sister got through until she had her accident. Now I do."

Bette was staring out at the old climbing town with its ancient houses and the square where the plane trees stood, green and dusty in their summer fullness. It was like going back ten years.

She gave the boy beside her a quick glance. What had he said about a sister? But of course, this must be Hugh, her other cousin. She was about to apologise for not recognising him at once when the taxi began to climb up a narrow street. Surely this wasn't the way out of the town and into the country? She was going to ask about this when they stopped, and her companion said; "Here we are. You'll be wanting lunch, I expect."

He was already out of the taxi and paying the man, before she could say a word.

They had stopped before one of the oldest houses in the street. Very old and picturesque, it had overhanging eaves and windows of many paned glass—casement windows heavily leaded. Her puzzled glance showed her that the lower rooms had been turned into a shop: on one side there was a display of wooden objects of all kinds, brightly coloured toys, cigarette boxes, and photo-frames, whilst the other showed one or two choice examples of filigree, brooches, necklaces, and, in the background, an old Jacobean chair on which was draped tapestry. Above the door clanked a sign depicting a blue jewel in a gold setting and the words "The Blue Talisman" in gothic letters.

Hugh, for it must be he, had already opened the door, and a shrill little bell jangled in the dimness.

He motioned her forward then shouted.

"All right, Clover, only me! She's come, thanks be!"

"I say, I'm sorry, I didn't realise you were Hugh," began Bette.

He looked puzzled. "Yes that's me, Hugh, come in and meet my sister."

"But why have you brought me here?"

He frowned. "It was all arranged wasn't it?"

"Er . . . yes. But aren't you taking me to Nicholas?"

He studied her now. "You're not Gladys Benson, then?"

"Of course not. I'm your cousin, Bette Danvers—don't you remember me?"

He went on staring. "You were a little fair thing of about ten when last we met but . . . of course I mentioned the name Ferndale, and naturally you thought . . . but are you going to the farm . . . I mean . . ."

He seemed to be quite out of his depth.

"I wrote to Nicholas saying I was coming."

Hugh looked depressed. "Well come in anyhow, Bette," he said with his kind smile, "guess there's some explaining to do all round."

A clear feminine voice came from a room beyond the low panelled shop. "Hugh, who is that? What is it?"

"Coming!"

Hugh began to explain quickly. "It's this way. Clover and I have struck out on our own. When Nicky was reported missing in Cyprus, we were staying at the farm which, of course, would have come to us. Then he did come back, luckily, after all. He was jolly decent really, he gave us some money to start this business on our own. I make things in my spare time when I'm not at the office, and Clover runs the curio side. We haven't been doing so badly, but last week Clover had a fall on the crooked stairs leading to the attic and twisted her ankle badly. She'd fractured a small bone in her foot so I had to get leave from work, and we advertised for someone to come and help for a bit."

"And you thought I was this person?"

"Yes. A girl called Gladys Benson answered. She works in the city and liked the idea of a change for the holidays. Well, she should have arrived to-day, she may still of course. Anyhow I'm glad we met after all. But come and see poor old Clover, she'll by trying to walk in if we chew the fat any more."

Relieved that the misunderstanding was cleared up, Bette followed him along the uneven floor of the shop to a cosy sitting-room beyond. It was shabby but it overlooked a very pretty walled garden. Lying on a settee by the window was a dark-eyed girl of about nineteen. Looking at her with instant liking, Bette could just remember the dark, rather serious thirteen-year-old who had come to stay at the farm with her brother all those years ago. At that time they had recently lost their parents and Clover had mothered her young brother with a care older than her years. Perhaps she would have got to know them better had it not been for Nicky who had been her ideal and her hero.

Now she went forward, hands out. "Clover! I'm not surprised you don't remember me after all this time."

Clover's serious eyes in her rather pale face brightened.

"Why, it's Bette, the little cousin! Not so little now! I don't know why we haven't kept up during all these years. Bad correspondents, I suppose. We must make up for all that now." She smiled. "I'd get up and make lunch but you see how it is. I *am* glad you looked us up." She gave her brother a quick glance. "Then Gladys didn't come after all, Hugh?"

"No, stupidly I went up to Bette here, never realised who it was and all but kidnapped her. Bette is going to stay with Nicholas."

Clover seemed astonished. "Bette, never! Did he ask you?"

It was Bette who looked embarrassed. "Not exactly.

I asked myself. He used to be so good to me when we were at the farm and I'd got nowhere to go for the next few weeks, so I just wrote off yesterday and came."

"So he's not expecting you?"

"He's expecting me all right. He'll have got my letter. I said I'd be over to-day," Bette told her with more optimism than she felt.

The brother and sister exchanged glances.

Hugh was frowning. "He's changed, you know. You'd scarcely recognise him. He even wears a beard to hide a scar he got. He's changed a lot."

Bette was looking so troubled that Clover said gaily; "Anyhow, stay for lunch, that is if you don't mind getting it yourself." She made a little face. "We were just getting on when this happened. Hugh, I heard two people try the door when you were out. Two!"

"I'll open after lunch."

"If you'll show me where the kitchen is and everything, I'll get it ready," said Bette.

"Can you cook?" asked Clover.

Bette struck an attitude. "I can, I've taken domestic science at school since I was twelve, and Mummy lets me help in the holidays."

"Good for you. Hugh, for goodness' sake show her where she can wash. Do the honours." She stirred uneasily and looked down at her bound leg. "I do feel a log, and I've got to stay like this for another ten days."

"Never mind," Bette consoled her, "I'll help."

Hugh indicated the way upstairs, and, after Bette had a good wash, she came down to the old-fashioned kitchen which lay beyond the living-room. Here she got busy and made a salad and omelettes for them all, laying a tray for Clover with commendable efficiency. In spite of the misunderstanding she felt quite cheerful. As she beat up eggs and watched the fat sizzling in the pan she could hear the others talking. During the last few years she had, of course, thought of her cousins and her mother had remembered them faithfully at Christmas, but Nicky had always come first. The cousins had both been to schools far less expensive than hers, and had spent their holidays on the farm. Now it looked as though they were very much on their own and having to strike out for themselves. Hugh already had a job and Clover, clever, gallant Clover, had taken on the shop. This much she had guessed. "Anyway, hats off to them!" she thought as she folded Clover's omelette with some grated cheese and set it, sizzling, on a hot plate. She was almost glad that the mistake had been made. Of course she must go on to the farm to-day, but first she would see what she could do for Clover, at least that she was comfortable whilst Hugh gave his attention to the shop.

She laid the table and brought in the food. Clover took her tray and was full of enthusiasm for the omelette.

"Hugh does his best. He may be the man of the family, but he can't cook," she said wryly.

Hugh grinned in complete good humour. "Even the potatoes refuse to soften for me and the cabbage took an hour yesterday," he confessed.

"What gave you the idea of starting a shop?" asked Bette as she handed round the salad.

Clover's explanation was simple.

"I've always been interested in old things, and Uncle used to take me to sales sometimes. Oh, he was a farmer and busy, but he loved sales, it was a kind of hobby of his. He taught me quite a bit about old furniture, jewellery, even pictures. Then, when Nicky was missing, we were still at the farm which would have been ours." She stopped. "Don't think we didn't simply howl when we thought he was killed, it was an awful shock. When we heard he was alive after all, it was wonderful. Then he came back and it was different. Perhaps it was silly of us to expect him to be just the same after all he had been through. But he's changed so much, hasn't he, Hugh?"

Hugh nodded. "I'll say he has! Same dark eyes, but they don't twinkle the way they used to, the same long-shanked figure, but kind of stiffer. Then, of course, a beard makes such a difference."

"Poor Nicky," murmured Bette.

"You needn't say that," Clover told her. "He's terribly self-sufficient and bossy now, and hard. Bette, he's gone so hard! But he wasn't bad to us. After all, Uncle left no will so he could have turned us off without a penny. Instead he asked me what I'd like to do. Hugh, all independent, went and got himself a job as clerk to an estate agent's here. I rather wanted to train as an interior decorator, but it takes money and time to train."

"But how did you get this place?" persisted Bette.

Clover finished her omelette with appetite. "It all happened so suddenly. Nicky had talked to me, and I rather gathered that he didn't want us around. Oh yes, Bette, he's got rid of all the old labourers, poor old Selwyn, and Hunt, even Mrs. Jennings the housekeeper. He has new people there now. He says he wants to give ex-service men a chance, but it was hard on the old people."

"Oh well, he paid them off with a lump sum," put in Hugh.

"Yes, yes, he did. He seems to think that money is all that matters. Anyhow about this place." She smiled reminiscently. "It belonged to an old chap called Zacharias. He was very old, and rather a dear—he actually wore a skull-cap. I used to come in and see his things and talk to him. Well one day after I knew I'd have to leave the Grange, I came in here. Nicky had told me he'd let me have three hundred pounds for my training; jolly decent of him really, for we hadn't any real claim on him. Well, as I say, I came in here, and found old Zacharias excited. His son had started a shop in London and he was leaving here to go and help him. He was looking for a tenant. To cut a long story short we talked it over and he let me have the good-will and the residue of his stock for three hundred pounds. Well I clinched it and believe it or not, Bette, I'm going to make a success of it."

"Of course you will and you deserve to," cried Bette. "I see you have started a side-line."

Hugh looked embarrassed and Clover gave him an indulgent glance. "Hugh likes playing about with wood and paint, and the toys and boxes and things he makes are quite a success; in fact so much so that sometimes I sell more from the left window than the right."

Later, when Bette examined the little carved animals, money boxes and cigarette boxes, she found that they showed both imagination and ingenuity. Hugh put some very good work into his hobby and if he spent a week carving a cigarette box, it was worthwhile when finished.

"I like doing them," he said.

"And once I can get out and about, go to sales and pick up things, *my* window will pick up," said his sister.

As Bette washed up after lunch she thought over what she had heard about her cousin Nicholas in some consternation. Of course the other two might be prejudiced, for after all they had been turned out of Grange Farm which they had grown to consider their home; and yet, Clover, as well as her brother, was too frank and loyal a character to harbour malice. No, obviously the experiences he had gone through in troubled Cyprus had changed the gay, attractive Nicky out of all recognition.

She would have regretted her impulse, that letter announcing her arrival, had it not brought about this new contact with these two cousins of hers. At least she would never lose touch with them again.

Hugh opened the shop after lunch. Hearing the chatter of children's voices Bette peeped in to see three small children arguing hotly over the choice of a yellow kangaroo and a grey crane. Finally the purchase was made and Hugh put the money into the big cash box, relic of old Zacharias's days.

"Customers," he said cheerfully when he saw her. Bette was putting on one of Clover's aprons.

"Do you think it will scare anyone away if I give the place a sweep and a dust?"

"I say, must you? I mean, will you? It's terribly dusty I know—Clover would faint if she saw it."

"Just you leave it to me."

The shop was very dusty but it was tastefully

arranged, with heavy old furniture, bureaux, bookcases, a very fine hope chest in the background, and an old refectory table by the window with its display of china, old ivory and brasses.

Bette got busy. She swept the shop well, uninterrupted as yet by customers. She found polish and a polisher and rubbed the stained floor until it shone, then she started on the furniture. She was polishing the ornaments when a customer did appear.

A rather garrulous woman wanted a small table. Bette, busy in the background, watched with interest as the woman priced every object in the place without buying a thing. Then her eyes fell on a small carved elephant.

"I'll take that, it will do for my little grandson," she said. Money changed hands, and Hugh deposited it in the cash box again.

"It's a left window day to-day," he said, then added with a grin, "Clover and I have little bets about it: left window days my days, right window days hers. Needless to say we feel more like celebrating for the right." He broke off. "My word, you've made a difference! Jolly decent of you, Bette. You've got a smut on your face, by the way."

Bette was by now feeling rather tired, but she was pleased with her work. The floor shone and the furniture looked twice as expensive, the china gleamed and she had even rubbed the semi-precious jewellery and brought a new sparkle to each piece. She was surprised to find that it was already four o'clock. Time for tea. Clover was busy crocheting little table-mats, another side-line, when Bette came in, smut still on face.

"You're being an angel," she said, "make tea of course, but I feel awful letting you do all this."

"S'pleasure," laughed Bette.

She made tea, cutting cheese and lettuce sandwiches, gave Clover hers, then carried a tray into the shop.

She found Hugh talking to a broad, fair-haired young man in tweeds. Hugh introduced him simply as Dr. Burton.

"He's coming through to see to Clover's foot," he explained.

The doctor shook hands. "I'm glad she's got someone to help," he said, "she's eating her heart out sitting there. Well, it won't be long now."

He went in to Clover and as he re-dressed her foot, he was told of the misunderstanding.

"Pity you couldn't have stayed," he said, "you'd have been a very present help in time of trouble."

"I'm beginning to think the same," said Bette, "but I shall come in and see Clover every day. It just depends what there is to do on the farm."

The doctor gave her a quick glance. "Grange Farm? Matter of fact I was out there this morning. One of the men sprained his back falling off a rick."

It was almost five when he had gone. Bette realised that, if she meant to get to the farm that day, it was time she started. As her only means of transport was the bus which stopped at the crossroad above Risley she decided to leave one suitcase and take the other with a few necessities.

When she went into Clover to say good-bye she found her looking rather distressed.

"Bette," she said seriously, "don't think I'm anything but disinterested, for I expect this Gladys Benson will turn up, but if you aren't happy at the Grange, you know you can come to us. You can have my room, as I am sleeping down here to save Hugh rushing up and downstairs."

"It's good of you. I wish I were staying, in a way, but I wrote to say I was arriving to-day, so I'd better turn up. Anyhow I'll be back often, and I do hope the London girl will be satisfactory." She gave Clover a rather shy kiss, stopped for a word with Hugh, busy painting some of his toys, then went out into the shadow and sunlight of the old street.

CHAPTER TWO

A COLD WELCOME

It was a good mile to the farm from the crossroads, and as Bette turned along the dusty lane which led to it, it was like walking back into her childhood. Presently she came to a gap in the hedge and stood looking through it at the old familiar view. There it stood, a cluster of many roofs with, beyond, the big tithe-barn. In the distance it looked every bit the same as she remembered it, only Bette felt different.

She had been all but a baby when her mother had carried her round the farm-yard to see her first chickens, and later she had roamed the place with Nicky. It was he who had shown her the oast house, let her play in the great shadowy barn where she had once found a tiny nest of field mice. Even now she could remember the nest with the microscopic mice and the little mother quivering at discovery. Nicky had been very gentle with the little mother mouse. It would be nice to see him again even if he had changed. For, reflected Bette wisely, people might change outwardly, put on a kind of defensive armour if they had been hurt, but inwardly they remained the same.

It would be fun to wander round the old place again; the low-beamed rooms, panelled and thick-walled, were gracious, for once the farm had been just the Grange with a moat all round it, a moat which now, in rainy weather, revealed a flow of water from some hidden stream.

Coming to the wide gates which lay open, revealing the rutted lane which led straight up to the paddock, she was changing her case from right hand to left, when a jackdaw fluttered in front of her from the avenue of giant elms on either side.

"One for sorrow!" So the jackdaws still nested in the fastness of the biggest elm.

The windows of the house showed red in the sunset, but the lower casements were shut, as was the door. The big lawn flanked by borders heavy with summer flowers was as she remembered it, but in the old days and in such weather, the door had always been open. In an indefinable way the house looked different though, windows shut, its twisted chimneys smokeless in the evening air—it was all so quiet and even the mass of outhouses beyond showed no sign of life.

Bette climbed the three steps to the porch. She remembered that they had always been gleaming white but now they were grey. She missed too her old memory of seeing through an open door, wide panelling, red flagstones set with rugs, and beyond, the garden at the back, complementing the beauty of the front with its massed roses and sweet-smelling lavender bushes. She rang the bell which was a long chain by the side of the door. Strange, but she had never done that before, perhaps because she had always been with someone or because the door had, in her memory, never been shut to her.

She waited: but no one came. She was still waiting in increasing impatience when a tall, gangling man with a red face and a pendulous nose came slowly up. He looked at the tall girl whose linen frock under her coat matched her eyes, and seemed surprised and not at all pleased. Then he said in a deep voice which came oddly from his thin figure and lean jaws:

"Who do you want? Don't take guests here."

Bette did not like him, he did not fit in with the quiet country scene. "I want to see Mr. Ferndale. I'm his cousin. He is expecting me."

"That so? Well, he's out at present. Better call again."

Bette drew herself up. "I'll wait, thank you. I've come to stay, he knows all about me."

"Huh," he looked her up and down, "first time I've heard of it. We want no womenfolk here." He had scarcely spoken when the door opened to reveal a woman. Bette turned and met colourless eyes in a colourless face. It was a plain face, long and thin-lipped, with the dark hair screwed back from the high bony forehead. Bette liked the look of her no better than the man, but at least her apron was clean. Presumably she was the housekeeper who had taken the place of the dear old, fat Mrs. Jennings.

"What do you want, dearie?" The voice was soft and husky, incongruous in the pale, unsmiling face.

"Mr. Ferndale is expecting me."

The pale eyes were watchful.

"Well now, I know nothing about this." She glanced at the man who stood by, watchful and suspicious. "Did the Boss say anything about a young lady, Beaton?"

"He did not. He'll be back any time, better have her in and wait." He strolled off.

Bette stepped into the hall. The red flags were swept but unpolished and there were no rugs. The panelling was dim, perhaps because the door at the end of the hall was firmly closed.

The woman continued to inspect her. "Unexpected, this. We don't look for company, not nowadays. Who may you be, dearie?"

"I'm Bette Danvers. Mr. Ferndale is my cousin."

"And he knows you're coming?"

"Of course."

"Come in then, he'll be back." She threw the door of the big parlour open. "Make yourself at home."

Bette put down her case and strolled to the many-paned windows, the woman watching her. There was something odiously familiar about the housekeeper's attitude which she resented. Not that Mrs. Jennings hadn't called her "dear" and "ducky" but somehow that was different.

The room, though neat and tidy, had that indefinable air of neglect she had already noticed. The big table stood as usual, eight chairs ranged round it, the book-case, with its masses of books into which she had peeped on rainy days, still stood in the embrasure by the deep hearth, the old piano occupied its place against the wall, and rugs lay neat and at right angles on the floor. But the floor was unpolished, the furniture lacked the glow of constant care and there were flowers nowhere; it smelt musty too, and faintly of mice, for the windows were tightly closed.

How quiet it was! Suddenly she thought of Hugh and Clover and wished heartily that she had never come. She was thinking this ruefully when the door opened and a tall man in riding-breeches and a khaki shirt came in.

She turned: another stranger! The dark eyes met hers above a neat, closely cut beard which gave him in her opinion a foreign or nautical appearance. He strode forward and, when she did not speak, smiled, his lips showing red between beard and moustache.

"So this is my long-lost cousin!" His tones were bantering but the eyes did not smile.

Bette stared. "I say, you're Nicky? I didn't know you."

"I could almost return the compliment, seven years is a long time." He broke off. "Sit down, my dear. Now look here, didn't you get my wire?"

She was startled. Yes, he had dark eyes, he had Nicky's fine figure, broad shoulders and lean hips, but he had changed.

"No, no I didn't! You see Auntie Joan went off and I didn't want to spoil her holiday so I wrote and came on here. I knew you wouldn't mind at this time of year. I can help. I'm quite strong."

"Impulsive, aren't you? You might have waited for an invitation. As it was I wired as soon as I got your letter, putting you off."

"Oh!" This was awful. She got up. "All right then, I'll go back to Fairham. I can stay with Clover and Hugh."

"You do that. Now, now, don't be hurt. You see this farm is now an entirely male community." He paused, then, as though she were a child, added a further explanation. " We are all men except for Mrs. Della and she doesn't count save that she's an excellent cook. Since I came back I've been running this place with the help of any ex-service men who need a helping hand—chaps down on their luck. I've got five staying here and a few lodged out, and it's working out very well."

"I'm glad."

"So you see I don't need help and I haven't time for a guest. You'd be dreadfully dull."

"It's all right, I'll go back to my other cousins."

"Oh them," he said, "so you know them, do you?"

"Of course, we were here together often enough."

"Yes, I remember now." He had changed in every way. It was the shell of Nicky she looked at now. It was as though Nicky had really died and been replaced by this cold stranger.

"I'll go back at once," she said, "do you know the times of the buses at the cross roads?" But Nicholas Ferndale was not listening to her, he stood by the window looking out, and Bette suddenly realised that a noise had been breaking the country silence for the last half minute. It was the sound of a plane.

Looking back long after, she was to remember that moment as significant. Had she gone only three minutes earlier, had she not prolonged that uneasy conversation with her cousin, she would have been away down the lane and eventually safe in Fairham. But they had talked, and now something was to happen which was to change her plans, and, if not her own life, that of others she did not even know as yet.

The noise of the plane tore the air now. Nicholas suddenly unlatched the window, threw it wide and put his head out. The sound of engines had risen to a roar, a menacing, uneven roar. Then it happened——

With the abruptness of a clap of thunder there was the sound of a terrific rending crash, followed by silence which was even more terrifying.

"Good lord! On the hillside," muttered Nicholas. He put his leg across the sill and was out, before Bette had realised what had happened; then she too clambered out, tearing the pocket of her dress as she did so.

On the hillside lay a shattered mass of wire and fuselage which had once been a plane; already the acrid smell of burning filled the heavy air.

Nicholas was racing across the paddock. He vaulted the fence to the sloping field where a couple of terrified horses galloped. Running swiftly, Bette followed and made up on him as he approached the shattered plane.

The smell of burning was strong. Nicholas climbed up into the cockpit and lifted the senseless figure which lay slumped by the instrument board as easily as though it were a child.

He saw Bette. "Help me disentangle his legs."

Frantically Bette did so and together they eased the unconscious pilot on to the grass.

"Run for it! The tank will explode any moment!" shouted Nicholas.

Bette did not listen but remained to help drag the

injured man as far away from the wreckage as possible. Soon shouts and running figures showed that the crash had been seen by the farm-hands. Three men arrived on the scene and Bette was able to stand by and watch as they carried the unconscious man to the house. One of the men, she noticed, was the one who had first accosted her, the others she did not know. She followed them into the hall.

A short fat man with the broad shoulders and heavy face of a boxer turned and said. "Bit awkward, Boss. Better get him to hospital."

"Later. Take him upstairs and put him on a bed. Get the doctor, Noakes, and be quick, we'll have the whole countryside on the field before we know it."

Noakes rushed off. Bette followed them up the stairs and watched them ease their burden on a bed.

"Take off his crash helmet," she said, "I'll get water. I know something about First Aid."

"All right, stand by!" Nicholas gave her a quick glance as though he had forgotten her existence. "Where's that Della woman?"

"I saw her go off for a walk," offered one of the men, a tall fair man with a coarsely handsome face.

Bette loosened the crash helmet and, with her cousin's help, undid and eased off the heavy leather coat. She propped pillows behind the head and noticed that a bruise showed lividly across the face and that one arm was hanging limply.

"Concussion, but I don't think he's mortally hurt," she said professionally and, as she spoke, the eyes of the man opened and he looked at them. He was quite young with lank fair hair and clear-cut features; the eyes were very blue, almost matching his Air Force uniform.

His eyes met those of Nicholas, who stood over him in silence, then surprisingly he said, "Why, if it isn't old Smiler! What you doing here, Smiler?"

He spoke clearly and his eyes looked alive and intelligent. Nicholas leaned forward. "Quiet, old man. Just lie still—you've had a nasty crash."

"If you say so, Smiler." He broke off. "Knew those engines were missing, just missed building . . ." He closed his eyes as though going to sleep.

"Well, do what you can. The doctor will soon be here," Nicholas said to Bette, and he stood by while she undid the man's tunic and bathed his head. She noticed a swelling by the neck and upper arm and decided not to do anything else until the doctor came.

As she worked she reflected wryly that it did not look as though she would return to Fairham to-night after all. Why, she did not quite know, but she did not like the idea of leaving the young airman here in the hands of the rough people who now lived on the farm. In Nicholas's hands? Absurd when she remembered the Nicky who had been gentle with a tiny field mouse, but it was so.

When the doctor arrived she was pleased if not surprised when he proved to be Dr. Burton who was attending Clover.

He merely nodded to her and gave her a little personal smile and a quick, "So you got here all right," before he attended to the injured man and made him comfortable.

This done he turned to Nicholas Ferndale who had remained in the room.

"Mind if he stays here a couple of days? I'd rather not move him yet, he's got a couple of nasty fractures and slight concussion. If you like I'll send round the district nurse."

Nicholas interrupted almost hotly. "For heaven's sake, don't send round a parcel of women here. My cousin is quite capable and the housekeeper can help as well."

Burton gave him an odd glance. "All right, Ferndale. As a matter of fact we're short of beds at the infirmary so you'll be helping if you have him. I'll be in again to-morrow, and we should be able to move him by Friday." He shrugged. "Saw the wreck just now, he doesn't know his luck."

"No," said Nicholas, "he doesn't." His tone was so queer that Bette glanced at him. He caught her glance and smiled, that fleeting smile which did not reach his eyes. No, the old Nicky had fled forever.

When the doctor had gone he put a hand on her shoulder.

"Think you can manage?"

"Of course I can. I do know something about nursing."

"Good. By the way," he glanced at the bandaged figure on the bed, "he may be a bit delirious so don't take any notice. Let him think he's in the hands of an old pal if he likes."

"Of course."

"Now we'll find that woman and see about food, and arrange for a room for you."

"If the one next to this is empty that would do," she suggested, adding, "it's the one Mummy used to have and I would be near if he calls out in the night."

He strode up the corridor and flung open the door. It was just as Bette remembered it, that room, with rather heavy old-fashioned furniture, and a big bed. The latter was unmade and the mattress was rolled up.

"I'll send Mrs. Della to make up the bed. The others all sleep in the left wing so they won't disturb you coming in late. If you should want me, I'm in the oriel room."

Bette nodded, "I know."

He gave her another of his sharp, fleeting glances then they went downstairs.

Bette saw nothing more of her cousin that evening. The woman laid the table in the parlour and brought her food—salad, cold ham, cheese and junket, and in spite of her nerve-racking evening, Bette ate with appetite. The woman's manner was still fulsomely familiar.

"You and me's got a job on seemingly," she remarked as, arms akimbo, she watched Bette eat. "Poor bloke, lucky escape 'e 'ad."

"Yes, Mr. Ferndale dragged him out."

"And you 'elped, I did 'ear. You modern gels is strong, I'll say that. Other chaps all came up when it was over, lot of feckless toughs them!"

Bette went on eating and wished she would go.

"I'll keep a look over 'im to-night, dearie, so you can sleep in peace. So, if you 'ears noises just stay put, 'twon't be the first bed I've watched by, or the last!"

With this rather depressing statement she took herself off, her pale eyes dull, her thin lips set.

Bette was very tired. It would be a good idea to go to bed early. To-morrow she would write to her mother and tell her of her change of plan, and write to Aunt Joan also, of course. How surprised they would be. Had it not been for the crash she would have been back with her younger cousins at Fairham. Now, as she found her way up to her room she wished it had not happened, even apart from the injuries suffered by the young pilot. She did not want to stay here. The Nicky she remembered was no more, his experiences in the Services had changed him out of all recognition. As for the friends, so called, who helped him on the farm, they seemed an odd company; Mrs. Della's expression "toughs" suited them well.

Before going to her room she peeped in at the young airman.

The doctor had given him an opiate and he lay still, his tanned face drawn in the fading light, but breathing evenly and peacefully.

She left him and was relieved to find that her bed was made and her suitcase brought up. She took out a few necessities only, for, as soon as the pilot was moved to hospital, she would leave too, though she felt she must stay until she knew he was in good hands.

The light faded and Bette slept. She came out of a cosy, dreamless sleep slowly, stirred, and turned to find moonlight flowing across the room through the windows. Something had wakened her but what?

She lay and the many incidents of the day before passed through her mind. The injured man in the room next to hers.... Had he called out? She listened, then, fully awake, sat up.

Surely that was the sound of a car in the drive? She looked at her watch, it was two o'clock in the morning. Then it came again, the sound which had wakened her, a dull whirring throbbing sound which she could not identify.

She got up and looked down at the silent garden below; nothing moved, but the whirring sound continued. It seemed to come from the depths of the house itself. Very wide awake now, and thinking of the helpless man in the room next door, she slipped on a dressing-gown and slippers and padded to the door. The door of the pilot's room was open and she crept in, relieved to find that he was still sleeping deeply. His forehead was warm and moist to her touch and he stirred and murmured something unintelligible. At least he was all right.

Coming out of the room again she had a moment of panic, as a tall figure split itself from the shadows, and a hand hard as steel caught her arm.

"What are you doing wandering round at this time of night?"

She choked back a little scream for it was only Nicholas.

"I heard a noise," she whispered, and realised as she spoke that the queer throbbing sound was now stilled.

"The dynamo's working, that's all. What made you get up?" His voice was hard.

"I only went to see how he was."

He let go her arm. "Such devotion to duty is touching. You go and get your night's sleep, young woman. Maybe you can be of use in the day but don't go wandering round in the night. You gave me quite a turn." His voice was light now, almost ingratiating. She slipped away into her room feeling shaken. For a moment she had hated and feared the man who was her cousin.

When she awoke to the sunshine of a new day her fears in the night seemed absurd and unreasonable.

She had heard a dynamo working in the night. Nicholas had been up and dressed at two in the morning, but a sick cow, or any of the eventualities of farm life might explain that. He had been abrupt with her but no doubt she had startled him. Perhaps he was nervy, after all he had been through a lot in Cyprus. Poor Nicholas, and yet the adjective "poor" did not in the least apply. Dressing quickly after a cold shower in the bathroom down the corridor, she went softly into the pilot's room before going down to breakfast. Mrs. Della was there busily tidying up.

"Oh it's you, lovey," she said, "just you go down and I'll have breakfast for you in two jiffs." The injured man stirred a little at the sound of voices but Bette was not needed. She wandered down and into the garden finding her way to the kitchen garden, where in the old days she, and sometimes Hugh, had gone in the early morning to purloin raspberries.

Here it was the same: pears ripened on the wall, the apple trees promised a burden of fruit come autumn, and the lines of gooseberry bushes, currant and raspberry canes, showed beyond neat rows of potatoes, cabbage and onions. Nicholas's workmen might be rough but some among them understood a garden. With a little smile she moved to the raspberries: she would pick a few for old time's sake.

She had reached them when a rustling and a scampering from something bigger than a juice-drunk thrush startled her. Bette could run fleetly: she went between the rows and caught the intruder by his shirt collar.

"Oy! What are you doing here?" she asked.

The small boy, who could not be more than nine, wriggled, then was still. He grinned a jagged grin showing gaps in his teeth.

"Hallo," he said. "Lemme go. I was only taking one or two, same as them big birds do. See that thrush, wobbly he is, he's been gobbling them away ever so fast."

Bette was amused. "I'll let you go, but you musn't do it again. After all, it's stealing."

Wide-set grey eyes in a dirty little face darkened.

"Stealin'! From 'im, 'im as treated my Grandad so bad!" he said. "Nay, guess he owes us more than raspberries."

"What's your name?"

"Bobby, Bobby Selwyn. I'm John Selwyn's eldest I am. There's Peter and Cedric, the twins, and M'randa and the baby, see."

"Quite a family!" The name Selwyn told her a lot. Old George Selwyn had been cowman here when she was a child and Clover had said that Nicholas had got rid of all the old staff.

"Where do you live?" she asked.

"In the village. Briar Cottage. Grandad's helping with Mr. Brent's cows, and my Dad," he broke off, "you'll never guess what my Dad is?"

Bette knew vaguely that old Selwyn had a family, but that was all.

"What is your Dad then?" she asked, getting ready

to show surprise. Bobby was obviously very proud of his Dad.

"My Dad's a perliceman, the village perliceman. You'd never fink that Briar Cottage was a perlice station but it is." He lowered his voice. "We've got a lock-up, but Mum uses it as the wash-'ouse, see!"

"How exciting," laughed Bette, "nice to have a policeman for your Dad." She stopped as she saw a tall figure moving by the paddock. "Off you go and don't let me find you round here again."

He grinned. "All right." As he turned to run off, he said over his shoulder: "I likes you, guess you're nice for a girl, see!"

Bette hurried away smiling—she liked small boys and there had been something rather endearing about the loyally unscrupulous Bobby. Her cousin approached her near the front door.

"Who were you talking to?" he asked lightly.

"A small boy I scared off the raspberries."

"That Selwyn kid, when I catch him he'll know it," he scowled.

But Bette felt gayer and happier this morning. She linked her arm in his. "Don't you remember seeing me and Hugh sneaking raspberries and always looking the other way?"

"Did I? More fool me. Come and get your breakfast. I've had mine hours ago, so you'll be in solitary state again."

She felt snubbed. Evidently it was no good reminding this new Nicholas of the old Nicky.

It was a good breakfast, well-cooked, and Bette enjoyed it sitting there in the quiet parlour. Mrs. Della had brought it in, but this morning her manner had been more in keeping with her appearance and she scarcely made any conversation.

After Bette had finished her meal she went upstairs. The door to the sick man's room was closed. She listened outside but as she heard no sound, she went into her own room to write her letters at the table by the window. As a rule she found self-expression easy but to-day she sat some time before finding the right words.

"Dear Mummy,

You will be surprised to see this address. As a matter of fact I couldn't go to Mavis as her sister had measles."

She stopped, remembering the lack of welcome here. Her action in wishing herself on Cousin Nicholas did seem impulsive, if not downright cheek. He had inferred that. She wrote on: "He is very changed; he has grown a beard and seems much more serious than he used to be. . . ." She went on to describe the crash, and in the end finished her letter in a hurry as she heard steps in the passage outside.

She got up and, leaving the letter to her aunt for later, went out. The door of the pilot's room was ajar and she had a glimpse of Mrs. Della's aproned figure just going down the stairs at the end of the passage. She crept in, for at first she thought he was still asleep, then she saw the eyelids move and a hand jerk restlessly on the sheet.

She moved forward and found blue eyes considering her with curiosity and a kind of amused relief.

"Hallo!" the voice was husky.

She sat down by the bed. It seemed to her almost as though she were greeting a friend among strangers.

The young man smiled. "Now, who are you, where is this place, and what is old Smiler doing here?"

Evidently he was still rambling.

"You musn't talk too much," she told him, "you've had a bad shock."

He grinned. "I'll say I have. But you're the only bright spot in my otherwise dismal outlook. What's your name?"

"Bette, Bette Danvers. This is Grange Farm—it's about eight miles from Fairham and it belongs to Mr. Ferndale, my cousin."

"Ferndale? Haven't met him yet, have I?"

"Yes you have. It was he who got you out of the plane. You thought he was someone else."

The blue eyes were thoughtful.

"You mean the chap who got me out was Ferndale?"

"Yes, of course."

"Come again! Last time I saw him was in very peculiar circumstances in Cyprus."

"He was out there. He was missing—captured by an Eoka gang, I think."

He made no remark to this. "But what are you doing in this outfit?"

"It was a bit of a mistake," she told him frankly, "I invited myself here because my holidays went wrong, but Nicky didn't want me. I'm only staying until you go to hospital, then I'm going to my other cousins in Fairham."

He smiled. "Now that's very nice of you, Bette."

Bette flushed a little. "What is your name?"

"Ian Trent. Squadron-Leader Trent at your service. Which reminds me, I'll have to get in touch with headquarters, if they haven't already got the dire news. Look here, see if you can get hold of your—er—cousin and say I must send a message to Hulton Aerodrome."

"You mustn't worry. They will have the news by now. The doctor went over to the plane, what was left of it, and took particulars with Nicholas."

"Stout feller." Then he looked troubled. "When did he say I could be moved? Don't like to inflict myself on people, you know."

"In a couple of days..." Bette broke off. Steps were coming down the passage, and a moment later Nicholas had entered the room. He entered briskly with a bright smile and a jaunty:

"Well, well, so he's awake and in his right mind. How are you feeling, old man?"

He stood over the bed and Bette, looking at the injured man, saw a medley of expression pass over his face.

He met Nicholas's eyes and said deliberately: "Quite all right. What's the game, Smiler?"

Bette saw Nicholas stiffen.

"Still wandering. My dear chap, my name happens to be Ferndale, Nicholas of that ilk, and the sooner you get that into your thick, apparently unbreakable head, the better."

There was a silence between them. Bette got up. Nicholas nodded to her.

"Yes, off you go. Tell Mrs. Della that her patient is awake and needs nourishment. I'll entertain him for a bit."

"Don't let him talk too much," cautioned Bette, her nurse's instincts well to the fore.

"No," said Nicholas, "I'll see he doesn't talk too much."

Was she imagining it or did his voice sound menacing, as though the words conveyed a hidden threat?

CHAPTER THREE

SOMETHING SINISTER

THE morning of that first day at Grange Farm passed on leaden feet for Bette. When she saw her cousin striding away across the fields to superintend the hay-making machine she returned to her patient.

He seemed to be asleep so she tip-toed away again and went out to the fields. Three or four men were gathering in the hay but she saw no sign of either Nicholas or the man called Beaton. The men stared at her unsmilingly, they were a sullen lot, unlike the cheery farm-labourers she was used to. Finally she went back to the house, finished her letter to her aunt, then went into the garden with a book. Mrs. Della came to call her to lunch and she was surprised to find Nicholas there, looking cool in flannels and an open-necked shirt.

"I'm driving into Fairham this afternoon," he said, "so I'm lunching early. Like to come with me and look up Hugh and Clover?"

She brightened. "Why yes, I would, but had I better leave Mr. Trent?"

"Who? Oh he'll be all right. I expect the doctor will blow in some time this afternoon. Whilst you're with your cousins you can see about staying with them."

"Oh I know they'll have me."

"I'm sure they will," he said, adding, "Indeed, I'm sorry I couldn't let you stay here but you see how it is. You'd be bored stiff after a couple of days; it's work, work and nothing else on a farm, and *I've* no time to entertain you."

"I quite understand," Bette told him quickly, "in the old days I suppose you were only a boy though you seemed grown-up to me. I guess you rather spoiled me."

He carved more of the excellent lamb. "No doubt. To me those old days are dreamlike in retrospect, I'd rather not talk of them."

Had his eyes not been so hard, his manner to match, she could have pitied him, but there was nothing pitiable about the wiry bearded man who now faced her across the big table. She would never, she knew, want to see him again once she had left, though the memories of that old Nicky would remain.

He told her to be ready at two when he would bring the car round. She had asked if she could take some flowers and fruit to Clover and he had agreed pleasantly enough. When she had got these, she went up to the pilot's room.

He lay very still, staring before him, and seeing her, he waved her forward. "Glad you came in. Look here, can you do something for me?"

He looked flushed and his eyes were feverishly bright.

"Of course, what?"

He paused for a moment, as though listening, then in low tones went on:

"Could you help me to get away from here to-night?"

"But you're going to hospital as soon as the doctor can get a bed."

"That may be too late. No, it must be to-night. Listen, can you wait until midnight then come and help me get up? I don't know my way about this house, of course. I'd want you to show me out and put me on the road to Fairham. Once on the road I shall be all right."

Was he wandering? Bette looked at his flushed face in consternation. "But you're not fit. Can't you get in touch with your Squadron?"

He gave her a troubled look. "They should have communicated with me long before now. Look here, you say you are going soon. Help me to get away first, you'll never regret it."

"But what is the matter?"

"A great deal. Wait, have you a pencil and paper?"

Bette got up. "I'll get some from my room."

"No, a scrap will do, just take down a telephone number. Piccadilly 0808. Got that? Ask for Smith, J. B. Smith, and if he isn't there ring Berkeley 050."

"What do I say?"

"Just tell him what has happened, and what you know, that's all you need do. He'll fill in the rest for himself."

By this time Bette was quite sure he was delirious, but she nodded. "I promise."

"Where are you going now?"

"Only to Fairham with my cousin."

"You're coming back?"

"Oh yes. I'll stay until you leave."

"Now about to-night, I must get away, so you will do what I ask?"

"Yes, I'll come in at midnight." She thought it best to humour him.

"I know it must sound strange to you, but I've got to get away and I can only trust you."

There was a sound in the passage. Had someone been listening at the door? When a moment later Mrs. Della came in, though, the woman looked as blank as usual.

"Mr. Ferndale is waiting in the drive, miss," she said, then to the man in bed: "Would you like a drop of tea, sir? I've just made some."

"Thanks I would, very much."

Bette turned and smiled good-bye. He returned the smile, but his over-bright eyes sent a message which said: "Don't forget."

Bette was astonished when she saw the car standing in the drive. It was a wide, shining American car and by far the most luxurious she had ever had the chance of driving in—an extravagant car even for a well-to-do farmer such as Nicholas Ferndale.

She sank down into the well-sprung seat.

"What a lovely car!"

"Not bad. She goes well, that's all I ask."

They swept along the country lanes, the car humming smoothly. It seemed that they reached Fairham in a moment of time, and once there he drove her straight to the shop in Fore Street.

He stopped but made no effort to get out.

"Won't you come in?" asked Bette.

"Thanks no, one cousin is enough at a time."

He smiled to take the edge off his words, but Bette

flushed as she opened the door of the now familiar shop.

The little bell tinkled and there was Hugh, as usual, tinkering with his home-made toys, big and cheerful as ever.

At once Bette felt better. It was like stepping into another world where everything was clean and sane.

"How's Clover?" she asked, "and did the girl turn up?" She broke off for Hugh was laughing.

"I should say she did." He turned and closed the door to the sitting-room. "Bette, she *isn't* a girl."

"But you said ' Gladys Benson '!"

He was staring out of the window: " Was that Nicholas? Some car. How did you get on with him?"

"I'll tell you everything when we're all together. Now what are you being mysterious about?"

Hugh grinned. "About an hour after you had gone, the bell rang and a little chap turned up, very nattily dressed, perky. I just stared at him, thinking he was a customer. He said, calm as you please, ' I'm Gladys Benson's brother. Do you think I'll suit, for I'm quite as handy as Glad.' Well, to cut a long story short, Gladys had had the chance of a holiday with a friend, but not liking to let us down, she sent Tim instead. He works at an office in the city and looks about fourteen, though he's eighteen, and, believe it or not, he can cook and do housework as well as any girl. He puts it down to Scout training. Yes, we're quite pleased with our temporary help but don't look surprised when you see him."

Bette laughed: "I won't, and I'm so glad you've got someone, though it looks as though I shall be coming to you this week-end after all. Hugh, I wasn't a bit welcome."

He gave her a quick glance. "Not? That's what Clover thought, though she didn't like to say anything to you. Our dear cousin isn't on the hospitable side." He broke off, "But come on in, as soon as Tim appears I'll put him in the shop. Another of his charms: he sells my toys at fifty per cent more than the marked price and gets away with it."

They went through and there was Clover, who brightened when she saw Bette.

"I say, it is good to see you—you know I've been worrying about you, silly of me! Fruit—and flowers, you angel! You must have got on the right side of our cousin."

She stopped as a slight dark youth with a thin cockney face came in from the garden.

"This is Tim, Tim Benson, our cousin Bette, Tim." Hugh introduced him with the pride of a conjurer.

"Pleased to meet you." Tim extended a capable hand.

"I'm so glad you came," Bette told him, "I hear you're very efficient."

"Do my best, miss. But that shop! Givin' things away, they were." As he spoke the bell tinkled and he nodded at Hugh.

"Just leave it to me, kids!" He hurried off importantly.

They all exchanged amused glances. "He's a dear," said Clover, "he makes us laugh because he takes himself so seriously. What worries me is that it isn't much of a holiday for him. You must take him to the coast to-morrow, Hugh."

Hugh nodded. "I'm going to take my holidays now, and I'll get him out after shop hours. Still he's enjoying himself, and he's an ideal salesman."

Clover eased her foot. " Put the kettle on, it's almost four. I know Bette is dying for a cup of tea." She turned to Bette. "I feel it in my bones that you've a lot to tell us."

Much had happened in the last twenty-four hours, so much that Bette found it difficult to know where to start.

"Well," she began, "he's different. He isn't like the Nicky I remember at all. Clover, I don't even like him now—I'm even a bit afraid of him."

Clover nodded. "I know, I felt the same. He can be nice but there's a kind of steely hardness underneath. Still he was only a boy when we knew him, though I suppose he seemed almost grown up because we were only kids."

"I suppose so." Bette hurried on. "But you don't know what happened. Yesterday evening, almost a moment after we met, a plane crashed on the farm land."

Hugh, busy making tea, almost dropped the pot. "I heard that one had come down. Gosh! Was it near the Grange? We heard that the pilot was injured and that he was staying with you. Is that true?"

"Yes, he is. He's quite young and awfully nice, but he's still very delirious. He seems to think he knew Nicky in Cyprus."

"What is his name?" asked Clover.

"He's a Squadron Leader, Ian Trent."

"Why, he's quite well known, he was trying out the N.5 at Farnborough last year, surely you've seen his name?" Hugh sounded excited.

"No. Anyway I'm staying until he is moved to

hospital. I help with him, you see, and Nicholas did not want a nurse."

"What a thrill for you!" sighed Clover. "Some people have all the luck."

"I don't know," confessed Bette, "I'm worried about him. He doesn't seem at all rational yet and he wants to get away from the Grange to-night—it's almost as though he's afraid of something."

Hugh gave a noise like a snort. "Squadron Leader Trent afraid, rubbish!"

"Well, he made me promise to come and help him get up and away late to-night, and I know he isn't fit."

"What is all this?" asked Clover.

Briefly Bette told them of her interview with him before she had come away that afternoon. "He must be delirious. He had a big bruise on his head, and—well, I can't think of any other explanation."

"Unless," interrupted Clover, "he has a reason to be afraid, and being sensible knows that he can't do much in his condition."

"Whatever do you mean?" cried Bette, then stopped as Tim came in cheerfully.

"Made a couple of sales, folks," he beamed. "Yes, that owl of yours, Hugh, and the Dutch girl. What did you want for them?"

Hugh, who had been thinking of other things, said vaguely, "Oh, the owl was three and six and the Dutch girl three bob, I think."

"I got five and nine for the owl and five bob for the Dutch dolly—and cheap at the price! You should see what they charge for such toys at the big stores."

Clover laughed. "You'll make our fortunes yet, Tim."

He sat on the edge of a chair and accepted a cup of tea. "What about an advert in the local rag? I've made one out." He drew a bit of paper from his loose tweed jacket, which was about a size too large for him. "Listen.

THE BLUE TALISMAN

Toys, toys, toys, for the boys
Dolls for the little dames.
Bring Mother to see our line in second-hand furniture,
Before they are going, going, gone!"

None of them could speak for a moment, then Clover said, " But Tim, the toys are only a side-line and the second-hand things are good stuff, not old junk."

"Never mind about that! You want customers, let 'em come and see it all. If they come for a doll for little Polly and end up by buying the grandfather clock, why worry!"

His dark eyes were bright as he looked around him. Then he got up. "Mustn't waste time. I'm fixing the right window in a tasty way." He grinned at them all and went out, whistling.

"Talk about a live wire," laughed Bette. "What kind of an office does he work in, for heaven's sake?"

"Newspaper office, Fleet Street," Hugh told her. "I expect he'll go far. But look here, Bette, about Trent? Are you sure he's wandering? And if you are, what about to-night?"

Suddenly, although it was quite warm in the sunny, pleasant room, Bette shivered. "I don't know. But the doctor will have been again by the time I return, so he'll probably have given him a sedative. He seemed very feverish when I left."

Clover mechanically took some bread and butter. "But suppose he is really in his right senses and must get away?"

"But why?"

Hugh frowned. "You say he knew Nicholas?"

"Yes, but he calls him 'Smiler', and thinks he's someone else. Nicholas seemed annoyed. It's all so queer."

"I'd say it's more than queer. Is it possible that our dear cousin got into some kind of trouble in Cyprus and Trent knows?"

"Impossible," Bette said, thinking of the old Nicky who had gone away. Then she remembered the new Nicholas and she fell silent for a moment. "Oh, Mr. Trent gave me a telephone number. I was to ring up if . . . if anything happened to him, I suppose." She brought out her diary in which she had scribbled down the number. "Here it is."

Hugh glanced at the numbers and the name. "J. B. Smith," he murmured, and then turned as Tim came rushing in again.

Tim looked at him. "What's this about the great J. B.?"

His interruption was hardly polite but they all turned to him eagerly.

"Who is he then?" asked Hugh. "Do you know him?"

"I should think so. He's a lawyer and well in with the police. He works for us—holds a kind of watching brief on the news, the legal side of it. The big boss thinks a lot of him. He's got a sort of flair for crime too: murder, arson, any jiggery-pokery—J. B.'s on to it before you can say ' knife '." He looked at Bette with new interest. "Friend of yours?"

"No, someone gave me his telephone number, that's all. Piccadilly 0808."

Tim grinned. "Our number—ten lines."

"Then the other Berkeley number will be his private one?"

"Yep, got a flat in the West End. Don't ring him unless you're on to something hot, he only deals with the big stuff." He broke off. "There's the shop-bell!"

When he had gone Hugh shrugged. "Did anything else odd happen?" he asked.

Bette nodded. "Well, the dynamo goes in the night—it woke me up."

"Where did it come from?"

"It sounded like somewhere in the house."

"Are you sure? The electric dynamo is in the shed by the tithe-barn. This is all getting queerer and queerer. Trent told you to ring this man if anything broke?"

Clover gave a little wail. "For goodness' sake, Hugh, don't start *talking* like Tim!"

"He told me that if anything happened—I suppose he meant to him—to ring this number, or the other one, and tell Smith everything."

"But his Squadron knows where he is. It doesn't make sense. I do begin to think he is wandering," said Hugh.

They argued fruitlessly for a while, then Hugh went back to the shop. Scarcely had he gone when the door opened to admit Dr. Burton, as cheerful as ever.

"Well, young woman, I left you to the last, and must hurry off now to my surgery," was his greeting. He nodded pleasantly to Bette as he examined and re-bandaged the foot.

"How soon shall I be able to walk?" asked Clover.

"In a week, if you take care."

Bette had been trying to broach the subject of the injured pilot, however it was Clover who did so.

"I hear you have another patient at the Grange Farm?" she said.

Dr. Burton nodded. "Yes, lucky chap to get off as he did."

"Have you seen him this afternoon?" asked Bette.

"Yes. I was able to tell him that I've got a bed for him in the Infirmary and we're sending for him to-morrow."

"How is he, do you think?" persisted Bette.

"Asking me to give away professional secrets! But of course you're helping to nurse him. Oh, he's all right, take a bit of time for the fracture to knit, otherwise he's as well as you and I."

"Didn't you find him delirious then?" cried Bette.

The doctor was preparing to leave. "Delirious? Not at all. Inclined to run a slight temperature that's all. No, Trent's all right. He's had worse, I gather."

He left them quickly without noting the look of consternation on both the girls' faces.

"So he wasn't wandering!" exclaimed Clover.

Hugh came in. "What's up?"

Bette stood up. "I must go back at once. Hugh, the doctor said that Ian Trent isn't delirious at all—you see what that means?"

Hugh's rugged face reflected their own consternation. "Good lord! What are you going to do? Help him get away to-night?"

Bette flushed. "It seems a dirty trick to play on Nicholas, and yet . . ."

Clover caught her hand. "Bette, I'm frightened. You will be careful?"

"Of course." Bette sounded braver than she felt. Suddenly she did not want to leave the pleasant, homely atmosphere here with the two boys and Clover, for the quiet and somehow sinister place that Grange Farm had become.

Before she left, she promised to return soon on the morrow to stay. Hugh let her out and at once began to shut the shop. Tim, helping with the shutters, gave her a nod; his sharp eyes seemed to have noticed something unusual about her good-byes, for he called after her: "If you want J. B. Smith, ring the Berkeley number after seven, but he won't like it unless it's hot news."

She smiled and nodded, then made her way towards the bus stop. The sooner she saw the young pilot and had another talk with him the better.

CHAPTER FOUR

STARTLING NEWS

THE Grange Farm stood deserted in the evening sunlight as Bette had seen it only yesterday. The large white cat which wandered about the place lay sunning itself on the lawn. There were no dogs. Bette thought of Mickey, the big retriever which had been a pet of the household in the old days—somehow a farm did not seem a farm without a dog.

To-day, however, the front door was open, although the one at the end of the passage was still closed. As Bette turned up the drive Mrs. Della came out and shook a mat defiantly at the sun. She greeted Bette with her usual familiarity. "Well now, and I thought we'd lost you. Past supper time it is, and the Boss taking his in the kitchen."

"I'll have a wash and then come down," Bette said pleasantly. "Don't worry bringing a meal into the dining-room."

"All right, miss, I won't; this 'ouse is too big for one pair of 'ands, specially with a lot of toughs in and out all day wearing big boots."

Bette was anxious to go upstairs. With Nicholas in the kitchen and Mrs. Della busy with her mats, she would be able to have a word with the injured man.

He must explain why he was so anxious to get away, and then she could make her plans for the night.

She hurried upstairs and saw that the door of his room was ajar. She knocked and, receiving no answer, went in. The room was empty. Bette stood on the threshold, staring, unwilling to believe her eyes. The bed was neatly made up, the table which had stood by it with glasses, water and medicine, had been moved to its usual place by the window. The room looked as though it had not been used for ages. Heart beating uncomfortably, Bette crossed the room and looked round her. Not a crease in the pillow even, showed where Ian Trent had lain; nor was there anything of his left there.

She rushed out and into her own room, threw off her coat and put down her handbag, then, not even waiting to wash, hurried downstairs again.

Nicholas Ferndale was in the kitchen. He sat where a place had been laid for him at the end of the huge table where a dozen people could dine at ease. As she entered he was delicately putting a piece of cheese on his bread. He popped it in his mouth and smiled his easy smile at her.

"Hullo, my dear, so you're back. Had a good time?"

She was too upset to disguise her feelings. "Where is he?"

He raised his brows. "He? Oh your patient. Really, my dear child, such interest is scarcely becoming in one so young. He has gone, as no doubt you have discovered."

"But he isn't fit! The doctor was moving him to hospital to-morrow."

The man shrugged. "What could I do? Not long after the doctor had gone, a chap, friend of his, came in a car and asked to see him. They had a long chat and, in the end, Trent went off with him. Seemed very anxious to leave my hospitable roof. Not that I'm sorry, we have no time for nursing here."

"Oh." Bette sat down at the place laid for her. Nicholas pushed forward salad and began to carve her some ham.

"Don't look so distressed. Most ungallant of him to go without saying good-bye of course, but there it is. We have our little disappointments every day as I expect you have noticed."

Bette tried to laugh. "Not such a disappointment really, I was only a bit surprised."

"Quite. Kind nurse goes up to grateful patient, grateful patient ungratefully absent."

She gave him a quick look. "Don't! You never used to talk like that."

His eyes flashed. "Like what?"

"Oh—sort of sarcastic."

He rose and folded his table-napkin. "Well, well, I'll relieve you of my presence. You'll be able to go to your cousins now. Everything is working out for the best."

"Yes, of course. I'll go to-morrow."

Alone, Bette looked uneasily around the great kitchen with its rafters and deep ingle-nook. Once it had been a friendly place, with firelight glowing and the rafters heavy with hams, bacon and the like: strings of onions and the acrid smell of herbs in little bunches had scented the air. Now the fire had been allowed to die down and the kitchen was full of shadows.

She told herself that she was relieved. Ian Trent had got away after all with a friend. Now there was nothing for her to do. And yet there had been something in Nicholas's manner which had unnerved her: he had seemed so pleased about the young pilot's leaving—he had been, in an odd way, triumphant.

Bette got up, her meal unfinished. Of course she was imagining things. She went upstairs again and, why she knew not, entered the empty room once more. The evening sun was flooding it and it was a vivid contrast to the gloom of the kitchen which faced east. She moved to the dressing-table where his tie and tie-pin had lain. They had gone, of course. The dressing-table was covered only by a dingy cloth but her eyes fell on the shelf above it, below the mirror. There was nothing on the shelf but a thin coating of dust—Mrs. Della was not very handy with a duster and it obviously had not seen one for days.

Then she saw the marks, marks such as a child will make with its finger on such a tempting surface. Someone had been scrawling on it. Words! She bent down to decipher them. "Got me. Old quarry, heard them. Tell Smith." The words scrawled in the dust tailed off. Bette stared at them, white to the lips. It meant that Nicholas had lied to her, that, for some reason, this man, a well-known pilot, had had to be got out of the way. The quarry? Yes, there was a quarry half a mile away. Her throat went dry as she visualised Ian Trent lying at the foot of one of the old workings: never to be found again. And she alone knew. He had managed by this childish device to tell her; he had taken a chance, but the chance had paid off and she knew.

Taking her handkerchief she dusted out the tell-tale marks, and as a door banged below, she hurried to her room, and sat on the edge of the bed trying to plan.

First she must telephone, there was one in the house but she dared not use it. The call-box at the cross-roads! She must go there and ring up that London number, the Berkeley number if she could believe Tim. "Ring J. B. Smith and tell him everything," that was what Ian Trent had said.

Feverishly she took out her bag and looked at the contents. What did a trunk call to London cost in the evening? She was not sure. First, the call-box then she would go to the quarry, but she must pretend that she was retiring for the night. Nicholas was sharp and she must act in an ordinary fashion.

She glanced at her watch. It was almost nine already. It would not be dusk until ten, and the moon rose at about midnight.

Quietly she got ready. She put on dark-coloured slacks and a thick sweater to match, for to-night she must move through the darkness unseen. She changed into rubber-soled sand-shoes and finally found her little torch which she slipped into the pocket of her slacks.

She strolled downstairs and into the garden. She heard men's voices from the back, but no one came into the pleasant garden. Forcing herself to whistle a light little tune, she began to stroll by the mass of tobacco flowers which, now that evening was come, had opened their yellow cups and were giving out their sweetness; in the distance a cow lowed and the old house once more looked gracious and inviting.

There was no sign of Nicholas. The white cat approached and began to circle round her. She stroked it, and it mewed, then stalked away, still mewing.

"What is it, puss?" murmured Bette.

The cat, tail-high, ran a little way, then waited. Bette who wanted to advertise her presence and her own lack of care for Nicholas to observe, followed her. The cat was stalking out of the garden to the line of stables at the back. Bette began to whistle again as the man Beaton came out of the stables and gave her a shrewd glance.

"Evening, miss, want the Boss?"

"No," said Bette, "I'm following the cat, she wants to show me something, I'm sure."

Puss had bounded across the yard and disappeared in one of the empty stalls of the stables.

The man gave a guffaw. "That cat's a scream. You go and see what she's got for you, missy."

Bette smiled and went into the stables. The white cat had sprung into a manger full of straw and there were five small kittens about a week old, their eyes still closed, wriggling and squeaking as they sensed their mother's presence.

"Oh, you proud puss, what a lovely mother you are," laughed Bette. She picked up a tiny grey and white kitten, not much bigger than a mouse and stroked its miniature head. The cat purred proudly. Bette stayed a little while, then, the fear and anxiety upon her once more, she made her way across the yard. A pump stood in the centre and, as she turned the corner from the stables, she saw Nicholas there sluicing his long bare arms under it.

He saw her and called. "Hallo, what you doing round here?"

She came up with mock eagerness. "The cat led me to her kittens in the stables. Can I have one when they are old enough, Nicholas?"

He gave her a lazy glance. "Kittens, eh? Sure you can have one. Come and choose it before you leave Fairham. You'll be going to-morrow, I take it?"

She nodded brightly. "Yes, to-morrow. Will it be all right if I go after lunch?" She took the pump and began to lever it.

"Of course. That's right, just a little more. Got some disinfectant stuff on my hands and arms helping with the cows, and I dislike the smell."

She went on levering the pump and watched the

water drip down on his arms; then she said something which afterwards she could have bitten out her tongue for uttering.

"Why Nicholas, what has become of that crown and anchor you had tattooed on your left arm? You used to be so proud of it. A sailor in Rye did it for you, remember?"

He shook the water from his arms and wiped them with a towel. All the time his steely eyes scanned her face.

"If you'd used as much Condé's fluid as I did in the army you'd know what it does to the skin," he said, then, "Off you run now, time little girls were in bed!"

She dropped the pump handle.

"Good night then. I am tired."

As she reached the house, her head was spinning. Did tattoo marks fade? Did they? If not . . .

She went to her room and stood staring out of the window. If they did not!

It explained much. It explained Trent's recognition of a man called " Smiler ", it explained why he had had to be got out of the way, it explained everything.

If those tattoo marks had not faded, if, as she suspected, all the Condé's Fluid in the world would not burn them out, this was not Nicky, not Nicholas Ferndale at all but another man masquerading as he, a man who had taken the real Nicky's inheritance and was using it for his own ends.

Suddenly she *knew* that this man was not Nicky, the gay and tender Nicky whom she remembered.

No, Nicky lay somewhere in the rugged Cyprus hills, asleep forever, that would explain it. Nicky had fallen perhaps to the gun of one of those EOKA snipers and this man, finding him, had assumed his papers and his identity. The likeness of figure and of colouring was there, striking enough to fool those who had known him only as a youth.

Bette began to tremble. It would not be so difficult. Nicky's father was dead, Hugh and Clover were easy to deceive because they had not seen him for so long, and he had evidently got hold of papers to prove his supposed identity. Why even old Mr. Blakely, the family lawyer, was dead, and the practice had been sold to another firm. It had been easy until someone came and recognised him, as had Ian Trent and herself.

What a fool she had been to exclaim over the missing tattoo! Yet he only thought of her as a child—she had appeared to accept his explanation. But now, if she meant to carry out her plans to-night, she must be more careful than ever.

The house was very quiet now but she must wait. The bogus Nicholas retired early or so he had told her, though she had seen him up and dressed at two in the morning only yesterday.

Something more than ordinary farm work was going on here, she knew that now; not for nothing had he turned off all the old labourers and brought in this uncouth gang of men.

She bunched up her thick coat and pushed it into the bed to represent a figure, then she took an old-fashioned flower bowl from the mantelpiece and laid it on the pillow, pulling the eiderdown up around it. Finally, she drew the curtains. It was a childish trick but it served: in the dimness, there did seem to be someone lying in the bed.

Still she waited. The darkness was now complete,

although later there would be moonlight. A wind had risen and swept across the hills, stirring the trees by the window and making odd creaks in the old house. She lingered another ten long minutes, then slipped out into the passage and down the stairs. From the kitchen at the end of the passage came the murmur of voices. She dared not use the front door; instead, she climbed out of the casement window in the parlour, and ran across the dark lawn. Once in the drive, where she could keep in the dense shadow cast by the elms she felt safer. She hurried up the lane towards the call-box at the end. Reaching it, she got her money out, dialled and asked for " Trunks ". Once she had pushed in the silver required, she stood very still, conscious of herself in the lighted box for anyone to see. Would there be time in the brief three minutes to tell J. B. Smith everything? She must be concise. As she heard the odd snatches of conversation on the wires of the operator putting her through, she tried to rehearse what she must say. Tim had said that this man was not the kind to help unless he thought it necessary.

"Trying to get your number," came the operator's voice. Then at last another voice " Berkeley 050." She pressed button A and gasped out, "Is that Mr. Smith?"

A calm, rather precise, voice answered: "Mr. Smith is abroad, and he will not be back until Saturday. Can I take a message?"

Bette's heart sank: it felt exactly like that, as though something lead-like sank in her breast. However she had to do something. "Would you tell him it's about Squadron-Leader Ian Trent," she gasped out quickly. "He has been at Grange Farm near Fairham and he has disappeared. Please ask Mr. Smith to help when he returns."

The precise tones repeated the message.

"Is that all, miss?" Did she sound so very young?

"Yes, that's all. No wait a minute!"

But the man had rung off.

Bette heard the door of the call-box clang behind her in something near despair. If only J. B. Smith had not been away! He had been her one hope.

Now for the quarry. She stood in the road taking her bearings. It lay, she remembered, due east from the farm but only about ten minutes' walk through the fields. In fact the quarry was on their land, and, in the old forgotten days, when Napoleon had threatened our shores, the owners of the farm had made quite an income out of it. Nicky had taken her there and helped her down to the old workings, chipped off part of the chalk, and shown her the fossils embedded in it. She decided to by-pass the farm, and to cross the fields, and so down to the cup-like valley which formed the quarry. Presently she found it so dark that she had to use her torch to find the little track she only just remembered, but, even as she did so, a faint glow showed in the sky as the moon rose slowly beyond scudding clouds.

She followed the path which wound through a little wood and on to rough common-land beyond. Then, she stood looking around her: down in the valley, she could see the farm which showed dark and unlit, but as she watched, a car drove along the lower road towards it and round to the back. It looked like a lorry though she could not be sure. She was almost convinced that the man who was pretending to be her cousin, not content with the inheritance, was planning some deep game of his own.

Those men he employed were not typical farm labourers, neither did they seem like ex-service men.

Still she hesitated, trying to summon up courage to go down to the quarry. She was afraid of what she might find there. Finally she forced herself to cross the rough ground until she reached the wide rutted track which wound up a hillside to the quarry itself. She followed this, walking in the tracks of the carts which had passed that way many years ago, until at last she came to the brink.

The quarry was like an amphitheatre below her. It stretched in a circle with the rails of the disused truck-line shining faintly on the quarry floor, before running off into a tunnel-cutting. Above the tunnel, the drop from above was the steepest. Bette stared down, trying to take in every detail. Nothing showed save the terraces of chalk, lichen and bramble, grass and fern. She must go down, though, and make sure, for that message in the dust had certainly mentioned the quarry.

She circled the arena to find an easy place for her descent. As a child, Nicky had helped her down, step by step, and she had enjoyed the thrill of it in the sunshine of a summer day. Now, alone, she was in an acute state of dread.

She found a low ledge which made a kind of step on to a lower one, then, face to the chalk-wall, she began the descent. The moon had risen higher and she saw suddenly that the rails of the truck-line came up the cliff-face a little to her left. She edged towards them, and, with the rails as support, she found it quite simple to climb down. Soon she was walking alongside the track on the quarry floor, with the steep walls rising around her, silent and deserted.

She looked around her, but there was nothing to be seen. She walked towards the tunnel and suddenly she came upon something she had not seen from above —a deep pool. It lay by the tunnel, black and menacing, with the water in it scarcely rippling. Coming round a pile of fallen chalk, Bette almost stepped into it.

Now she remembered that Nicky had told her how, when the workings had been given up, a small quake had disturbed the ground and it was fed by some hidden stream. He had even warned her that it was extremely deep. "Not my idea of a swimming pool," he had said, the gay, laughing Nicky.

As she stood there, suddenly it was as though he was with her, the real Nicky, not the steely-eyed and bitter pretender.

"Now, Bette, my girl, take a hold on yourself." So near did he seem that, when she heard a low sound she was not afraid. It was more than a sound, it was a voice.

"Who's that?"

She turned and looked around. "Who is it? Where are you?"

"The tunnel—quickly."

The pleasant voice, now sounding urgent and distressed, was familiar to her. She hurried round the pool and peered into the darkness of the tunnel. She saw the rusty lines and then, with a sudden start of terror, made out something which looked like a bundle of rags, ten feet away from the entrance.

CHAPTER FIVE

THE NINE LIVES OF IAN TRENT

SHE switched on her torch. Ian Trent lay there, fully dressed in his uniform and leather coat which were soaked through.

She rushed to his side. "Oh . . . oh," was all she could say.

He managed a smile. "Good kid, you saw the message. I heard them talk of a quarry and here I am."

"But how is it that——?"

"I'm still alive? Chaps at the station always say I have nine lives, I'll say this proves it. They brought me out in the car and chucked me over the highest part, I thought I was finished until I hit water."

"The pool, yes."

"I managed to swim out and on to dry land and dragged myself here."

"Didn't they come and look for you?"

"Not at once. They had scarcely got me over when they were interrupted—some countryman, a poacher no doubt. By the time one of the chaps came down, I had scrambled here. They think I'm in the pool, food for fishes if there are any."

She was looking at his drained white face anxiously. "I must get help. I can call up the police from the box at the crossroads."

He nodded and a tremor went through him. She felt his head and found it was burning with fever.

Suddenly, in desperation, she remembered something. Not more than five minutes' walk from the quarry was an old shepherd's hut where, in the old days, blankets and food had been kept. Before she left the injured man she must make sure he was at least dry. She told him what she was going to do, and he nodded; even his short talk with her had exhausted him.

Afraid no longer, only intent on what she must do, she climbed up the quarry again. Standing on the top, breathless, she looked across the common and saw the hut standing near a little copse of trees. She raced towards it. The door was padlocked, but in her present state of mind this meant nothing. She found a big stone and, after several attempts, smashed in the window. She rolled the sleeves of her woollen jumper over her hands to avoid cutting herself on the broken glass, and scrambled in.

Her heart leapt when she saw a bundle of blankets on a packing-case by the window, and a man's coat hanging on a nail over the door. She took it down and discovered that there was a whisky flask in one of the pockets. It looked as though someone was using the hut—possibly those toughs at the farm. She took the blankets, the coat and the flask, and clambered out of the window.

She almost risked life and limb climbing down the quarry again, but desperation helped. When she reached the tunnel she was panting.

Trent stirred uneasily but managed a smile. "Well, little lady, what a lot of trouble I'm giving you."

She handed him the flask. "Look what I found in the pocket of this coat." She opened it and he took a long sip.

"Thanks, that should help," he gasped, a little colour returning to his face.

"Now," she directed, "let me help you ease off your coat. You can't lie in those wet things." She helped him, careful of the bandaged arm. "Now get off as much as you can and keep these blankets round you over the coat. Promise?"

"I'll manage, trust me. But what are *you* going to do?"

She ticked off her plans: "First call the police, then the doctor. They'll have you in hospital in no time and then . . ."

He broke in: "Did you do anything about that phone message I told you about?"

"Mr. Smith is away abroad until the week-end. His man took a message."

"He would be, drat him!"

She watched him anxiously in the dim light from her torch. "Now can I trust you to get off all those wet things?"

"You can, lady. Off you go." She turned to go when he called her back. "About that man, your cousin?"

"He isn't."

"So you've found that out. Well, don't go back to the farm. Go to those cousins of yours in Fairham, straight there, even if you have to walk, understand? If old Smiler finds out what you've done to-night—well, he can be a very nasty customer."

"I know. I'll go back to the village, then perhaps I'll get a lift to Fairham. I won't go back to the farm."

"Be careful, child."

"I will."

She left him. She had done what she could, now she must get help for him. She climbed up the quarry, taking the shallowest slope. She had reached the top when a figure showed by some bracken. Had she been seen by any of those men? Her old terrors returned. Then the figure dashed towards her, a little figure after all.

"Why miss, what you doin' here?"

It was Bobby Selwyn of all people, Bobby Selwyn up to mischief, no doubt, at this time of night, for he looked round him surreptitiously before he asked: "You alone?"

"Yes. What are you up to, Bobby?"

He grinned. "Looking for Billy, he's my ferret. I lost 'im down a rabbit hole. Don't say nuffin, miss, Dad and Mum don't know I'm out and it's ever so late."

She was thinking quickly. "I won't tell on you, Bobby, but you can help me."

"Yes, miss?"

"Listen, tell your Dad to ring Dr. Burton and to go to the quarry. There's an injured man in the tunnel who needs help."

Bobby stared at her. "But I dursn't. Dad doesn't know I'm out. I dursn't."

"Oh Bobby, it's a matter of life and death. Your Dad will be glad to know."

Suddenly he grabbed her arm. "Some 'un's about," he whispered hoarsely, then dived behind some bushes and disappeared.

His ears were evidently sharper than hers. Now, silhouetted against the sky some fifty yards from the quarry edge, she saw a figure: one glimpse of the lifted head and dark, jutting, bearded chin was enough.

It was the man who called himself Nicholas Ferndale and he musn't find her here. She threw herself down behind some brambles which scratched and tore, her heart thudding painfully.

She heard the sound of steps approaching. The man seemed to come within a few feet of her, hesitate for a second, and then move on. For the moment all hope of gaining the road and the call-box had gone. She knew instinctively that she was in deadly peril. She must remain hidden until he had gone. She waited, trying to visualise the countryside: less than half a mile away began the forest of Wychwood, but, even in the old days she had never ventured into it alone, for it stretched for many miles out to the west, and children had been known to get lost in it.

No, she could only wait, then slip down to the road. She must telephone and get help for Ian or he might die. She had told Bobby, but he was only a little boy and afraid of his father, she could not rely on him.

The wind was rising and clouds scudded across the moon. Sometimes the countryside was deeply dark, sometimes a place of light and shadow. All was still again—the watcher seemed to have gone. But what had brought him out? Nicky the farmer might have been looking for a stray lamb or sheep, but this was not Nicky but an unknown, sinister stranger who had taken his place.

Had he discovered her absence? She could wait no longer. She got to her feet, and, keeping in cover of the sparse bushes, skirted the quarry. About a hundred yards across rough commonland lay the road; she could picture the call-box as though it beckoned.

It was very dark as cloud dimmed the moon. She

stumbled over a rabbit hole and fell, then abruptly moonlight filtered across the landscape again and she saw the figure of another man, down on the road. She turned in terror, and saw yet another coming from the other side.

"Better encircle the quarry!" came a familiar voice.

"O.K. Boss!"

Bette's breath began to come in quick, nervous gasps: she was being hunted. Her flight had been discovered and she had been traced here. Her only hope was to double back and try and gain the woodland. She heard the crackle of dry bracken fifty yards away, then, mercifully, the moon was dimmed again. Her only hope was to get away in the brief darkness. Half-doubled, she made towards the distant trees.

During the next bitter minutes she was to know what a hunted animal feels like: the rabbit and the stoat, the fox and the hounds, the stag. But they had swiftness, and the instinctive guile and scent of all wild things.

Her rubber-soled sandshoes made no sound on the soft turf. If only the darkness would hold! For a time it did, and the wind blew more strongly so that she could hear no noise from her pursuers. She had gained the top of a rise now; in front of her was a stretch of level grassland and beyond that the forest. If only she could reach the forest, she could elude the searchers until the light came.

She turned: below her she counted five pin-points of light hovering round the quarry—obviously her hunters were using torches. But she had reached the meadowland—she could smell the over-sweet scent of meadowsweet, feel the thick grass under her feet.

Then abruptly, the clouds cleared again and the place was flooded with moonlight. A shout reached her ears. She had been seen. The trees looked deceptively near and she began to run towards their shelter. They were all coming after her now. Panting, her heart thudding in her breast, she ran on. She made for a great oak which stood on the fringe of the woodland.

Steps were getting nearer: she turned round to see a tall thin man gaining. But now she had reached the oak and beyond showed the shelter of massed bracken and saplings—the tangle of the forest. Avoiding a path, she plunged straight into the undergrowth. Branches whipped her face, tore at her slacks, but she did not stop. All was dark here under the trees, and the rustle and startled cheep of a disturbed bird came to her. If she rushed on like this they would hear her. She threw herself down and lay hidden by bracken. She peered out. Some distance away was a little glade, dominated by a huge oak-tree, a very king among trees.

The man who called himself Nicholas appeared, behind him walked Beaton.

"Where are the others?" asked the former.

"Beating round the meadow."

"Call them in. She's made for the forest. I saw her. She can't have gone far."

"Probably quite near."

The man she now hated and feared gave a muffled curse.

"Beat round the bracken. She must be somewhere near. All round the verge within a hundred yards, and keep your ears open. She mustn't get away. Understand?"

The shadows seemed to move like live things as the moon was clouded again and hid them from view. She heard them tramp away. Feeling more than ever like a trapped animal, she waited in her shelter of bracken, not daring to move lest they heard her. But if they beat up all the undergrowth, they would find her—then what could she do? All was still again and very dark. She seemed to have been lying there for hours, although it was probably only a few minutes. Then she heard a low voice.

"That's right, Bully, go it, Bully. . . ."

Perspiration broke out, and her scalp tingled as there came a sound of snuffling and scrabbling from the undergrowth fifty yards away.

"Oh, so you did get him. Good, he'll find her." It was the bogus Nicholas's voice.

They had got a dog, perhaps even a bloodhound, to track her down. She was finished.

It was then that her wits, sharpened to acuteness by her danger, came to her rescue. Subconsciously she had heard for some time the faint tinkle of a stream which ran not more than a few yards from her down the glade. If she crossed it that would put the dog off the scent, this little she knew.

Leaving her shelter she ran, uncaring of the rustle she made, and stepped into the brook. It was wider and deeper than she expected, and her feet went down into a foot of water before she churned to the other side. Beyond was the glade and the oak. The oak—Oak Apple day! In a flash came the old story. How Charles II, three hundred years ago, had sought refuge from his pursuers in just such a giant oak. She stumbled across the moss and almost fell on one of the big pronged roots. Here she hesitated: the shouts of encouragement to the dog sounded very near.

She ran her hands along the bowl of the tree feeling for a low branch up which she could climb. She found one at last. The ensuing scramble and the mad climb seemed to last for a long time. She could now hear the baying of the dog as, losing the scent, he ran madly up and down the side of the stream. At last she was on the first bough. She climbed higher and felt massed leaves around her, then higher still until she sat astride a high branch. The tree rustled and whispered around her, but she was safe.

The moon came out again and the glade below her showed deserted. The dog still bayed but now in the distance, and she could hear men's voices shouting encouragement. She eased herself on her bough and tried to take stock of the situation. She must stay here a good while until they gave up the hunt, but dared she, knowing about Ian Trent's terrible plight?

She was bruised, her slacks and jumper were torn, and a long scratch on her face irritated her. Suddenly she felt so weary that she almost fell from her uncomfortable perch. She held out her wrist watch and read it in the moonlight. Only a quarter past twelve. Soon the moon would set and then she would have her chance, but she must wait.

It was hard to wait, for, apart from her weariness and general discomfort, she kept seeing Ian Trent lying helpless and uncared for. She alone knew of his urgent need, she alone knew that Nicholas Ferndale was not all he seemed. She thought of her mother who did not even know where she was yet. No one knew of her present plight, yet here she was within a mile or so of police and homely God-fearing folk.

She shivered as though she were in the middle of nightmare, the kind incurred by a high temperature.

High temperature! Ian Trent who knew too much was still in the quarry. His head had been hot and his eyes over-bright. She must get help to him. She stirred —one of her feet had pins and needles, and she didn't feel she could hold out much longer.

Steps sounded on the path, lighter steps followed.

"We'll have to wait till daylight, Boss," came the voice of the man Beaton.

They sounded just below her. Bette could scarcely breathe.

"To think a bit of a girl could disappear like that!" It was the bogus Nicholas.

"The 'ound trailed us back to the quarry-edge, her scent was there right enough. Gone over maybe, Boss, and good riddance, I'd say."

"I tell you I saw her make for the forest."

"Tis a mortal bad light with the moon in and out—maybe 'twas your imagination, Boss."

"Imagination! I haven't got one," snarled the other.

They tramped away at last. Bette looked at her watch: nearly twenty to one. Need she still wait? She made herself wait another ten minutes. Soon the moon would be on the wane and she must somehow get to Fairham.

She descended shakily from her refuge. Once on the ground, she swayed a little and stood against the giant bowl. "This won't do, my girl," she told herself.

She decided that she would not go round by the quarry, to the road; that would be asking for trouble.

The Boss might have left watchers there. Instead, reaching the verge of the forest, she moved south, keeping in the shadow of the trees. She thought herself very careful and was just about to cross the meadowland to the road when, abruptly, a figure appeared by the distant hedgerow.

Panic-stricken, Bette plunged back into the trees. She found a path which wound up and down between hazels and bracken and she ran along this deeper and deeper into the forest. Suddenly an unexpected dip in the ground found her unprepared in her wild flight. She fell, rolled a little way then lay still, the fear and exertion of the last few hours had been too much for her and she lost consciousness.

When she came to herself it was to the sound of the restless cheep of birds. She sat up. Her head ached from a bruise she had got in that sudden fall, but she was alone and a silvery light showed in the east. It was dawn already.

She staggered to her feet: the dawn of a new day and she still had not telephoned. True she was safe, but she was alone in the green forest with only the birds for company. She was feeling very dizzy and ill. Mechanically, she brushed her torn slacks and made a vain attempt to tidy her hair in which leaves and bits of twig were sticking. She realised suddenly that her purse was missing—it must have fallen out of her pocket during her wild rush. She had failed to make that call—she had failed Ian Trent.

She stood still, listening; they would start looking for her again soon. She must get to the road now, though it was barely five o'clock and no one would be on it yet. Even without money at least she could telephone the police. She looked around her—a narrow path wound away through endless trees. Which way had she come?

Trying to throw off her weakness, she followed the path and she walked on until she came to another path winding to the right. Which way should she take? She turned and went back by the way she had come. It must be a different path. She took a turn to the left again. Last night she had scarcely noticed direction but this must lead somewhere. Surely she could not have come far from the outskirts of the forest. Lost in an English forest! It seemed absurd, and yet there had been stories of children, at least, getting lost in Wychwood.

"I mustn't panic," she told herself. "If I follow the sun rising from the east, I can bear south."

She tried to be sensible and follow her own advice, but, in her nervous condition after her fall, her head ached and she still felt dizzy. The forest glades swam before her, the paths wound in and out like a maze, and an hour had gone before she realised that she was definitely lost, that in her wild race last night she must have run farther into the depths of the forest than she knew, and that she was now even less able to help the injured man who waited there in the cutting of the quarry, his life at stake.

CHAPTER SIX

THE HOUSE IN THE WOODS

BETTE was near despair. It seemed to her that she had been walking up and down narrow paths for an eternity when, coming down a steep rise, she saw roofs beyond the trees, the roofs of a house. The relief gave her new hope and she hurried on. She found herself in a glade with rough fencing beyond. She approached it and now through the trees she could see the red roofs of a pretty, old cottage. She circled the fence and as she did so she heard a woman's voice calling.

"Monty, Monty, Monty, where are you?"

There was a sound of barking, then through the bracken towards her came a small black and white terrier, tail high, eyes bright. It pranced up to her and began to circle round, still barking.

She held out her hand for it to sniff but it retreated round the fence. Bette followed and now had a good view of the cottage which was stoutly built with two deep eaves and a porch heavy with honeysuckle. The little lawn before it was close-shorn and the garden a medley of late summer flowers—phlox, asters, golden rods, dahlias and even roses. Standing on the lawn, greeting the truant Monty with chiding affection, was a little old lady. She was dressed in a wide black skirt over which a bright apron showed and, looking at her jutting chin and rather long, thin nose, Bette was reminded of the witches in a book of fairy tales. Only a black conical hat was needed to complete the picture. Yes, in fairy tales anyone lost in a forest would meet a witch or a dwarf or a charcoal-burner. Bette felt that she was living in some kind of fantasy outside the reality of ordinary life.

She leaned against the fence and suddenly trees, cottage, garden, the figures of the old woman and dog whirled around her. She must have made some kind of noise, for, after what seemed a long while, she felt two wiry arms round her and a pleasant, light little voice said, "You poor child! Can you walk? Now, round this way. Here we are."

The little woman scarcely came up to her shoulder, but her arms were strong as she led Bette towards a narrow gate in the fence.

"That's right, now up these steps and into the house. You mustn't mind Monty, and Bess is only growling because of her puppies."

Bette found herself in a low-beamed room. She was made to sit on a deep settee by the casement windows, and immediately a soft wet nose insinuated itself into her hand. She looked down at a beautiful spaniel. The place seemed to be full of dogs but, when the faintness passed she saw that there were only . . . only! . . . five, Monty the terrier, the spaniel Bess, and three silky puppies which rolled on the rug.

The old lady returned and put a cup of hot tea in her hands.

"Sip this, my dear. It's hot and sweet and I put plenty of milk in it. Don't talk, just sip it up."

Bette sipped. Never had a drink tasted so good as that hot, sweet tea. She leaned back and the room became clearer. It was untidy—books lay everywhere, and flowers had been put into an odd assortment of vases with no particular arrangement as to kind or colour, but Bette noticed that the rugs and curtains were spotless and that the floor and furniture were well polished. Altogether it was a most homely little room, peaceful and safe.

The little old lady sat down and took up some knitting.

"I'm always up early because of the animals," she said. "How do you feel now, my dear? Soon you must eat something and I've got the kettle on so that you can have a good wash."

"I got lost in the forest last night," Bette explained, "then I had a fall and only came to myself when it was light."

The bright blue eyes in the pointed face were shrewd but kind.

"Lost—I can see that, child. Where do you come from?"

Bette hesitated. Dared she tell her extraordinary story to this old lady?

"I was staying at Grange Farm."

"Tut-tut—that's miles away. You have indeed got yourself lost, my dear. What will your people think?"

A quick shiver, not unobserved, passed through Bette. "I expect they're looking for me now," she said with reason. "Where is this?"

"This, my dear, is Bracken Cottage. Very much off the beaten-track, I'm afraid. A small lane leads to the road which ultimately reaches Penvale. I know I'm isolated but I have my dogs for company and don't want to change." She smiled. "I used to be more active, of course, but now my dogs, my books and a weekly expedition into the town suffice me."

"But you must be lonely?"

The other shook her head. "I'm used to it, and I have my work; I will show it to you later." She got up. "Now you must have some food."

"Are you on the phone?" asked Bette.

"No. I'm afraid the nearest is at the Hall, a mile away. But don't worry, it's very early yet. Have some food, then, when you are rested we will see what can be done about communicating with your people."

She bustled off, leaving Bette to the company of Bess, who was proudly licking her puppies.

Presently the smell of frying bacon reached her and she realised that she was very hungry. Her hostess laid a place on the littered table, and brought in bread and marmalade. Then she placed a huge plateful of bacon and egg before Bette, who attacked it with vigour. "I shall be eating you out of house and home and you're so far from the shops," she apologised.

"Don't worry about that, child, I shan't starve. My grocer calls twice a week for his order."

She talked lightly of this and that and, when Bette had finished, showed her a neat little bathroom and told her to take off her slacks and jumper.

"I'll brush and mend them for you whilst you have a nice wash," she promised. "You don't want to frighten your friends!"

Bette enjoyed that wash almost as much as the food. She gave herself a quick rub-down and then put some ointment, which the old lady had provided, on her scratches and bruises. She combed her fair hair into some semblance of its usual smoothness, and called.

Immediately the old lady returned with her clothes. The tear in her slacks was beautifully mended and her jumper brushed too.

"Yes, I'm handy with my needle," said her new friend, "Come and see my handiwork."

It was already past seven and Bette was anxious to be off. She was dreadfully anxious about Ian Trent, but she had perforce to be polite and, when the old lady led her into a small room off the lounge, she followed. Here, in rows on a shelf, on a table, on chairs, were dolls, rag dolls of every type; from gay ladies in satin frocks to big-eyed golliwogs in checks and stripes.

"My work," said the old lady, "I send them to the hospitals. Some I sell, but not often. I have means, thanks be."

"Why they're lovely!" cried Bette, taking up a dainty doll with pink skirts and blue ribbons. "A cousin of mine carves toys and animals, and sells them." She stopped—Hugh and Clover seemed so far away.

"What is the matter, my dear?"

"I didn't tell you before because I didn't think you'd believe me. I came to stay with my cousin Nicholas at Grange Farm and after I got there I discovered that it wasn't Nicholas at all but a man pretending to be him. He knew I knew, and they were trying to catch me last night. They were tracking me down with a dog, but I climbed an oak-tree like Charles II. And an airman crashed on the farm-land and he recognised the other man. So they threw him over the quarry. He fell into a pool of water so he wasn't killed but he's very ill and I must telephone at once. . . ." Out it came in an incoherent jumble of words, and even to Bette's own ears, it sounded melodramatic and unreal. The old lady put a cool hand on Bette's forehead.

"Now, now, dear, you're running a temperature. Yes, I know the signs. To bed you go, in my niece Josie's room. Rest, that's what you want, and some good physic."

Bette met the concerned eyes. The old lady didn't believe a word. But what could she expect?

"But it's true, *honestly*, that's why I must telephone!"

"All right, dear. Mrs. Benson's boy will be over with the milk soon. I'll get him to ring up Grange Farm. Meanwhile you must rest." She took Bette's arm firmly. "Now up the stairs. Just slip off your clothes and I can lend you a nightdress."

Bette drew away. "You're very kind, but I must go now. And, by the way, my name is Bette, Bette Danvers."

"Yes, Bette. Mine is Amelia, Amelia Benham, Miss. Now I may be only an old woman but be guided by me. You were lost and frightened in the woods; give yourself a little time to recuperate and I'll get in touch with your people at Grange Farm."

Fear, real fear, showed in Bette's face, fear which almost scared the old lady.

"You mustn't, you mustn't! It's just what you musn't do! That man won't rest until he finds me. Don't you understand? I'm the only one who knows, and I've got to get help for Ian Trent."

Monty gave a bark at her voice which was so high and excited, and Bess nuzzled her puppies to her with a warning growl. Bette, almost but not quite pushing Miss Benham aside, hurried out of the lounge and through the front door.

Miss Benham trotted after her, uttering little ejaculations. "My dear, come back! You're not fit to be out! Oh dear, oh dear, such a business! What can I do? Child, stay here with me. I promise I won't tell anyone if you don't want me to, but you're ill, very ill —fever and an excited imagination. My little nephew used to be like that."

Bette turned in the doorway. "Thank you for everything. One day I'll come back and really explain, but I must go now."

She ran out into the sunlight, down the little garden path and through the gate. Beyond wound a country lane rutted and uneven, beyond that would be a road, the road to Penvale. From there she could get help from the police for Ian Trent and eventually reach Fairham and her cousins. She ran down the lane towards that road.

It was a lonely road, part of the forest lay on one side and on the other were ripening cornfields, though there was no sign of the farm to which they belonged. In spite of the food and her short rest Bette was suffering from the effects of her dreadful night and she soon became breathless. She was glad when she had left the forest behind her and turned to a road with hedges on either side.

She had been walking for more than fifteen minutes when, abruptly, the hedges gave place to walls of grey stone with the trees of what seemed a considerable park, beyond. Remembering Miss Benham's mention of the Hall, she skirted this wall with new hope, until posterns showed and to one side a lodge. However, this was empty and shuttered, the small garden untended. Still there was a wide drive which must lead to the house itself and she hurried along it. A few minutes later she came to a fine Georgian house with tall windows which shone in the morning light. The place was deserted—a trio of blackbirds strutted on the lawn. She hurried to the front door under a fine porch and rang the bell. It was the kind of house which boasts at least a butler, most certainly a telephone.

She rang once then again, and, receiving no answer, skirted the terrace. No doubt, as it was still so early, the servants would be at the back. Stairs led down from the terrace and a flagged path wound to a yard flanked by stables and outhouses. Another humbler door gave upon this yard. She was about to knock when steps sounded behind her. A stout woman, hair in a scarf and wearing an overall, had come round the corner. She stared at Bette in astonishment.

"Well now and what would you be doin' round 'ere so early in the morning?" she asked.

Bette had not told her story to incredulous ears for nothing. "There's been an accident," she explained, "I want to telephone please, if you'll let me in."

The woman was interested at once. "An accident now? On the road is it? Well, and you do look white. But I'm sorry, miss, Sir James is away in London and when he goes, he takes his staff, times being what they are and servants so difficult, and all's shut up here."

"But there's a man injured, I must telephone."

"Well now, I'm sorry. I'd help you if I could, but I only comes in to air the rooms like."

"But surely you could let me phone?"

"Nay, that's just it. It's cut off, always is when the master goes away. Comes of 'im being in the public eye like, and people trying to get 'im 'ere when they should try London. So you see miss, it ain't no use."

"Oh . . . thank you." Bette turned away. She felt hopeless. The woman shouted something after her, but she was hurrying to the drive: she had already wasted a precious quarter of an hour.

If, a few days ago, anyone had told her that England, which looked so small on a map, had so many isolated spots she would not have believed it. She had already been lost in a forest and now, in her desperate need, she could not find anyone to help her or contact them by ringing up.

She regained the road and hurried on in desperation. The old lady had mentioned Penvale as the nearest town, but had inferred that it was some distance away. Now Bette wished that she had asked her more about it and not rushed out like that.

Then suddenly her luck seemed to turn. She had scarcely walked a hundred yards when she heard the sound of an engine behind her. She turned: a light van was coming down the road, moving at a rattling pace. She stood to one side and waved. The man at the wheel drew up and she saw a stolid red face under an oily cap.

"Are you going to Penvale?"

"Yes, missy, want a lift?"

"Thank you, I would be obliged. I . . . I've lost my way."

She got in and he drove on. She scarcely looked at the fellow, her mind busy: Penvale at last, a place with police whom she could get in touch with at once. It would not be long now.

Then the man spoke. "Seems I've seen you somewhere, missy."

She glanced at him. "Oh, have you?" she said

vaguely, thinking that he was merely talking for talking's sake.

"Yes, round at the farm, some relation of the Boss's, aren't you?"

Bette went cold. It was almost too much, surely fate could not treat her as badly as this.

"I'm afraid I don't know what you're talking about."

He grinned. "That so? Oh well, guess he'll be pleased to see you again."

She tried hard to look unconcerned.

"Anyhow I'd like to stop at Penvale first," she said, "I have to see someone."

The man put his foot on the accelerator and the light lorry sprang forward. Fields and hedges flew past. They were going uphill now, and at the top the thin spire of a church steeple could be seen.

"Maybe you do at that, but I think I'll pass it by," he said. "I've an idea the Boss will want to see you, and soon, see! Yes, I've an idea that I've had a stroke of luck this morning. 'I'll take out the van,' I ses, 'and run round by the forest early mornin',' I ses. 'Much good that 'ull be,' he ses, very bad-tempered the Boss at cockcrow this morning. But I had my way and here we are." He was grinning. Bette stared at the flying road. Dared she jump? They had reached the top of the hill, and now they raced through the quiet streets of a large village. Was it Penvale? But soon they were past it, and on a country road once more, a road which she knew only too well, was taking her back to Grange Farm and that man whom she dreaded and feared more than anyone she had ever met.

She had escaped through the hideous night, tried and failed to communicate with the outside world, and now here she was a prisoner, facing she knew not what.

Suddenly she stood up in her seat with a wild notion of throwing herself out. Better face injury than the unknown terror before her! The man put out a sinewy arm and jerked her down.

"None o' that now!"

Driving with one hand, he held her firmly down on the seat. Tense she sat, but as they neared the farm, she knew that all was lost.

Her face was very white and her grey eyes dark with fear. The man drove right up to the door and sounded his horn. At once Beaton came running round the house followed by two other men.

The driver waved. "Got her! She accepted a lift—can you beat it? Where's the Boss?"

Beaton gave Bette a brief glance.

"Gone off in that posh car of his. Don't know where. What shall we do with 'er?"

"Best keep her safe till he comes. It's up to him then. Get Mrs. Della!" A fair, good-looking youth with empty eyes hurried off.

Bette felt sick, just sick—the smell of oil and petrol seemed all around her. When she was helped down she had to lean on someone's arm, so dizzy did she feel. Then Mrs. Della was there.

"Let her be, she won't get away now," she said firmly.

"Where you going to put 'er?" asked Beaton.

Mrs. Della considered. "Best make it the vaults till 'e comes," she said.

The vaults! The big cellars under the house which, even as a child she had not been allowed to explore. Someone, it may have been Nicky, had said there were rats there. But now, so ill did she feel, that, when Mrs. Della held her arm and led her into the house, she came like an automaton. Even if she had been fit and well, it would have been no good trying to escape, and she felt far from fit and well.

Mrs. Della was surprisingly kind. She brought her hot water in the bathroom and once there Bette disgraced herself by being extremely sick.

The woman tended her without speaking, then said: " 'Tis a pity you ever darkened these doors, both for your own sake and others who'll be nameless. Now, dearie, I'll do my best to make you comfortable so long as you keep quiet."

Holding Bette's arm she finally led her downstairs again through the kitchen, then down some stone steps. They were going to the vaults. Bette, feeling better, now that the nausea had left her, struggled back, but the woman propelled her forward and banged the door behind them.

"Down here—guess I'll put you in the strong room," she said. At the head of the stairs she switched on a light and below were the famous vaults. The low ceiling was supported by age-old pillars, for this part of the house dated to the time when the Grange Farm had been a manor house with a moat. The woman led the way across and beyond a pillar they came to a heavy iron-clamped door. Its old mortice lock had been taken off and a new modern one put on it. Taking a queer-shaped key from her pocket, Mrs. Della applied it and the door swung ajar.

"In you go, and presently I'll bring something for you to eat. There's a bed here ready, it's had its uses before."

The room was not large, and the rough walls had been repaired and reinforced by concrete. In one corner stood some packing cases, in another an up-to-date safe, by the end wall was a camp bed with blankets and a pillow neatly folded on it, whilst high above was a grating through which faint beams of sunlight filtered.

"Now," said Mrs. Della, efficiently thumping the pillow and mattress, "just have a little lie down and I'll be back with some food." Her pallid face showed no emotion at all, but then it never did.

Having made the bed, though, she turned at the door. "Once I had a baby girl, guess she'd have been just about your age by now."

Bette started up. "Mrs. Della, help me. I'm so frightened."

Fear was reflected in the pale eyes. "Don't talk like that. I haven't much left in this world, but I value my own skin. As I said, 'tis a pity you came here." She went out.

Left to herself, Bette moved round her prison restlessly. She thought of Ian Trent, helpless, perhaps dying. She had failed; in spite of her escape last night she had failed. No one knew he was in the quarry and he had been ill when she left him.

And what of herself? Hugh and Clover would be waiting for her to-day. What would they do when she did not turn up? She had told them enough to make them suspect more. Yes, and she had given the message to J. B. Smith's servant. She paced towards the grating; beyond showed a bank covered by some climbing plant and there was a sound of trickling water. This part of the vaults was by the moat. Stretching up, she felt the grating but it was only about a foot and a half square and the bars held firmly in the deep walls.

She sat down on the bed, too weary to do anything. When, later, Mrs. Della brought her food and set plates and cutlery on a little table, she did not speak. There was bread and good strong soup, and she was surprised to find herself enjoying it. Having eaten she lay down, hands behind head, thinking, thinking.

When would he, whom his associates called the Boss, return? She was very afraid, for she knew that she was in his way and that she knew too much. But hours seemed to pass and no one came. Once she heard voices and the sound of a car, but this part of the vaults lay at the back of the house and the green bank of the old moat obscured any view she might have.

The sun was moving round to that side of the house and its light became stronger. She was lying listlessly on the bed when she noticed something in the wall opposite which she had not seen before—that the wall was not old and of stone, but comparatively new and little more than a partition, and flush with it was a narrow door.

She got up and approached it curiously. An odd-shaped latch showed in it and a lock. She tried the latch and the door moved inwards with ease.

What lay beyond? She hesitated, staring into the darkness which met her. Then the brief light from her own prison showed her something familiar and ordinary to one side of that door—an electric light switch.

She pressed it and sudden bright light dazzled her. She was looking into a big room, four times the size of the one behind her. In it were machines, and in the centre a large table clamped to the floor. There was a familiar look to the machines and she stared at them in growing realisation of what they must mean here, underground, in an innocent-seeming farmhouse.

In a revealing flash she knew the secret of Grange Farm, the explanation of the sounds she had heard the other night. She understood now and the fact that she had stumbled on the truth because Mrs. Della had, perhaps mistakenly, put her in the vault room, made her even more apprehensive.

She switched off the light quickly and stepped back into her prison, closing the door behind her.

The day was passing but it seemed a long time before Mrs. Della again came in with food: tea, salad, and ham.

"Has he come back yet?" asked Bette.

The woman was not to be drawn. "You'll soon know."

She went out and seemed to make a more than necessary business of locking the door behind her. Bette tried to eat, but she had no appetite.

How was Ian Trent? Had even the man of nine lives managed to survive the immersion and shock for another twelve hours? The question tortured her even more than her own plight. She felt very near despair, helpless and alone.

CHAPTER SEVEN

HUGH TAKES STEPS

"You gotter do it, Bill, you gotter. 'Ere's fourpence."

Bill Roberts stared at young Bobby Selwyn doubtfully. He had a certain healthy respect for P.C. Selwyn but he didn't see why he should take orders from Bobby, who was some two years younger than he was.

It was nearly nine o'clock in the morning and the village street was deserted save for a few women going to the bus stop with their baskets. Bill had been going off for the day on a fishing expedition when Bobby had intercepted him and asked him to ring up his own father, the village policeman, with the news that there was an injured man in the quarry on the Grange Farm land.

"What's it all about, young 'un?" Bill asked now.

Bobby looked pale, for he hadn't had much sleep the night before.

"I've told you, 'aven't I? I was out, and my ferret got lost. Ever so late it was when the young lady, her that's staying at Grange Farm, stops me and tells me to get my Dad as there's a man in the tunnel of the quarry hurt bad, see."

"Well, why didn't you?"

"Me tell Dad! 'E'd be mad at me if he knowed I was out last night. I can't, see, and if I rung 'e'd know my voice. You needn't give a name, just tell 'im, that's all. Dad's got to do somefing about it. Look 'ere, it's a matter of life and death, she said so. Just ring up our number from the call-box by the Post Office, 50 it is, and ask for Dad. 'E's still in, I know. Just say a man's 'urt in the quarry, get a doctor, see."

Bill stared at the younger boy, then took the coppers.

"All right, but I don't like it," he said. Bobby watched him go to the call-box, then made himself very conspicuous by the door of the village police station which was his home. He heard the telephone ring, he heard his father's voice, then, not long afterwards, P.C. Selwyn appeared, got his bicycle and made off in the direction of the quarry. Bobby waited. If that girl's story were true his Dad would ring from the crossroads phone for the doctor and ambulance.

Time passed. Had that girl been pulling his leg? She looked ever so nice, had been nice about the raspberries, but you never could tell.

Then he saw Dr. Burton driving towards the quarry, and some time later an ambulance jingled its way through the village and people came out to stare.

Bobby pretended to be very busy in the garden, but, by midday he had heard the news which was now flying from mouth to mouth in the village. An injured man had been found in the quarry; some said it was the pilot from the crashed plane, which didn't make sense.

His mother was quite excited. "Quite on the map we're getting. First a plane crashes on the Grange land, and now a man murdered in the quarry."

"Murdered, Mum?"

"I haven't got the rights of it yet, but seemingly he's badly hurt and your Dad is investigating how he got there."

Bobby allowed himself a swagger as he turned away. "Guess I could tell a bit if I cared," said the swagger, but Bobby didn't dare say this aloud. Still, he had done his best, when he saw that girl he'd tell her. Nice girl, she hadn't given him away about the raspberries and her tale *had* been true.

The shop off the High Street in Fairham was busy that Saturday morning. Clover lay restlessly crocheting her little table mats and listened. She could hear Hugh's voice, and Tim's, and sometimes the latter would come in with news of a sale.

"Chap after that big desk. Says he'll come back. I asked eight pounds ten for it."

"Tim, I got it for three pounds at a sale. We painted it and Hugh mended the locks."

Tim grinned. "I'll allow he may beat me down, but it's all but sold."

Hugh was gratified because a cigarette box he had spent some time and care on had pleased a visitor and sold for half a guinea. Children were his chief customers though, and he would spend quite a time letting them handle his little animals and even showing them the uncompleted Noah's Ark he was busy on.

Clover, in spite of the fact that their business seemed to be taking a turn for the better, was worried. Bette had promised to come to them to-day, but when the morning passed with no sign of her or news from her she thought of Bette's story with anxiety. Had she managed to help the young pilot get away in the night? It was all very odd and disturbing. She wished that her cousin were safe with them.

It was past midday and Tim was already clattering

away with plates in the kitchen, when Hugh appeared.

"A wire," he announced, "addressed to you."

She opened and read it quickly, disappointment and consternation showing on her face.

"It's from Bette. Listen. '*Plans changed am returning London this morning. Love Bette.*' "

She handed it to Hugh. "She might have come and seen us before leaving."

Hugh put it down. "Handed in at Penvale. Cousin Nicholas must have run her there to catch her train."

"And after all she told us. Hugh, it does seem queer."

"Where would she go in London?" pursued Hugh. "Her aunt and mother are away. I'd give something to know what has happened to that Air Force chap too."

Tim appeared, apron round his thin waist, carrying a tray. "Chops and onions, my hearties," he said, "and I managed chips." He broke off. "What's up?"

"Bette isn't coming," Clover told him, "and we were wondering about the pilot too."

"But I thought it was all arranged," said Tim, "I wonder if she rang up J. B. What *was* it all about?"

Hugh and Clover exchanged glances. Tim was sharp and it would do no harm to see what he thought, so they told him everything. How Bette had come to stay with Nicholas, self-invited, received a cold welcome, and remained to help nurse the injured airman.

"And he seemed to be under some illusion about Cousin Nicholas. He thought he was someone else, and he asked Bette to get him away last night," finished Clover. "Yes, and it was he who gave her this Smith man's number."

Tim who had been eating his lunch with appetite, put down his fork. "Then Trent thought this chap Nicholas Thingummy was someone else?"

"Yes, and Dr. Burton who attended him said he was not delirious but in his right mind."

Tim nodded. "I get you. On the top of that he's anxious to get away, and tells your cousin Bette to ring J. B. and tell him everything. I don't like it." He brooded over a chip potato, then repeated, "I don't like it at all."

Clover looked distressed. "Anyhow Bette will be safe in London by now."

Tim gave her a sharp glance. "You sure about that?"

"What do you mean?" asked Hugh.

"Let me have a glim at that wire."

Hugh passed it to him. Tim studied it.

"Handed in at Penvale, ten-thirty this morning. Where is Penvale, by the way?"

"It's a large village beyond the forest on the other side of Grange Farm."

"I see. I still don't like it. People of Trent's type don't get the wind up about nothing. They don't usually make mistakes about people either. If he says it wasn't Nicholas Thingummy but someone else, I'd say you could take his word for it."

"Tim!" Clover's voice was high.

"I mean it. But then you must know your cousin. Wait, how long is it since you saw him?"

"Almost eight years. He was only a boy of sixteen then."

"When this chap came back were you sure it was Nicholas?"

"Why yes, the beard made a difference but the height and colouring were the same. Besides, he has the farm—he must have proved his identity. As it was we never questioned it."

"Did Bette recognise him?"

"Why yes, I think so. Of course he's changed but we put that down to all his experiences in Cyprus. You know he was wounded and was missing for a whole three months."

Tim turned to Hugh. "What do you think? Say you'd met him in a railway carriage, on an escalator in town, in any old crowd, would you have gone up to him and said 'Hey, Nicky!'?"

Hugh looked thoughtful. "No, I wouldn't. He was just a boy when he went away and afterwards although his height and colouring were the same, there was the beard. . . . But of course he was settled at the farm and we just sort of took him for granted. . . . No, I don't think I'd have recognised him as Nicky."

Tim went on eating. "There you are. Question is, what has become of your real cousin and the pilot chap?"

They were all silent.

Finally Hugh got up. "When we shut up shop this evening we'll go to the farm and have a gander."

"That's certainly an idea," said Tim, "and if there's anything queer, know what I'll do?"

"No."

"Ring up J. B."

He finished his meal, and helped clear away; then he went to open up the shop again. He was whistling as he did this in a thoughtful kind of way, but his eyes were very bright.

More irritated by her enforced inaction than ever, Clover waited through the afternoon. Dr. Burton would be in and she would be able to ask him a few questions. He was late, however, and when he did come he seemed a little troubled and disinclined to talk.

"Your young cousin arrived yet?" he asked.

"No, we had a wire to say she's gone back to London."

The young doctor gave her a quick look. "Is that so? A bit awkward. I can't get hold of Ferndale—he seems to be away from the farm, so I thought she might have been able to tell us something."

"Why, what has happened?" asked Clover.

He hesitated. "Oh well, it will be in the papers soon enough. A very queer thing. You know, of course, about that Air Force chap who came down by the Farm?"

"Yes, of course."

"Policeman at the village there got a mysterious telephone message. It was a boy's voice, saying there was an injured man in the quarry tunnel. Selwyn, that's the village policeman, went to investigate, and found a man unconscious and in a high fever. I was called and now he's safe in hospital. That man was Ian Trent, the pilot. I visited him only yesterday afternoon. How he came to get into the quarry is a mystery."

Clover's heart was beating fast. "Can't he tell you?"

"No, he can't. He's in a bad state, though I hope he'll pull through. He'd fallen in the pool there and crawled out, but another mystery—someone had given him a coat and blankets. Lucky we found him, though only just in time."

Clover stirred uneasily. "I do wish I wasn't tied down by this leg."

The doctor smiled. "You'll do, only another few days."

He left her, looking very preoccupied himself, and she could scarcely wait to call Hugh, who appeared anyhow, as soon as Dr. Burton had gone.

"And how's the gammy leg?" he began when Clover broke in.

"What does it all mean? Listen, Hugh, to what he's been telling me." She went on to tell him what had happened to Bette's pilot, as they called him, and as she told him Tim slipped in from the shop, scenting something unusual.

"What did I tell you!" he said.

Hugh turned on him. "Well, what did you tell us? Oh, I know it's all pretty queer but you couldn't possibly foresee this."

"I did, I think," said Tim modestly, "Stands to reason that if this pilot chap knew more than the so-called Nicholas liked, he'd got to be put off the map, see!"

"But what about Bette?" cried Clover. "Of course we got the telegram, but what happened? Remember, she'd promised to get Ian Trent away last night."

"Someone got in first," said Tim. "Frankly I'd like to know a bit more about your cousin's whereabouts too. This Nicholas may have thought she knew too much."

"Tim! You mean she may not have gone to London?" Clover had gone white.

"Anyone can send a wire." Tim broke off. "There goes the shop bell. Anyhow Hugh and I are going over to the farm this evening." He paused. "By the way, the customer I sold the desk to said he'd come and collect it after six. I wonder, if we moved the settee to the door, if you could sit there and watch for him? I'll leave the shop door open. The desk is paid for so all you have to do is to see he gets it and you can tell him—he's quite a decent chap—to lock the door after him."

"All right," said Clover tonelessly. The thought of waiting uselessly whilst the boys were out at Grange Farm was already making her feel restless. Still it would be a change to have the settee moved and see out into the shop.

When this was arranged she lay back comfortably. Had she not been so anxious she would have enjoyed this new prospect of the shop there before her, with its lines of now shining furniture, its odds and ends of china and semi-precious jewellery, and, at the end, the two windows which met the sunlight and showed the passers-by so clearly since Tim had been busy with a wash-leather.

The two boys went off almost on the stroke of six. Hugh had managed to borrow a bicycle for Tim from the shop down the road, and they rode off looking intent and serious.

For a while Clover lay still, neither reading nor crocheting. She looked at the shop with pride, thinking how attractive it was. She started pricing the goods mentally—anything to keep out of her mind the fear that something had happened to Bette. And distrust of the man she knew as Cousin Nicholas started growing—suppose Tim had not been exaggerating after all? It was true that he had returned a changed man, but with his dark eyes, dark hair, and tall slim figure; physically, surely, he was the same. Perhaps in the army he had got into some kind of trouble and the airman had known him under the nickname of "Smiler". But then Ian Trent had been found all but dead in the quarry on the farm land, and Bette had seemed almost afraid of him. Suppose Tim, although no doubt an avid reader of crime fiction, had not been exaggerating?

She looked down the shop once more. It was getting dimmer now, a place of long shadows and flecks of infrequent sunlight as the evening lengthened. The whirr of cars and the distant sounds of feet on the pavement were reassuring, but she started when Becky, the big tabby who had been there when they took over and remained, jumped on her covers with a low whicker. Clover was stroking her when the door-bell jingled and a tall figure entered and closed the door firmly behind him. A tall figure with a square box under his arm. Clover sat up at once. It was Cousin Nicholas, the person uppermost in her thoughts. For once he had not brought his car or else he had parked it farther down the road.

He paced the shop casually, now and then pausing to take up a little ornament, glancing round him, even making one of Hugh's tumble clowns do a somersault across the display table.

At last he moved towards the end.

"Hallo there! Hugh, Clover, anyone in charge?"

It took Clover an effort to answer him. There was, or so she imagined, something menacing about that cat-like tread, and the tone of his voice, even though slightly amused, seemed to hold a threat.

"I'm here, Nicholas," she called, trying to make her voice sound casually welcoming, "you'll have to come to me. Hugh and a friend have gone out cycling, so I'm in charge. I expect Bette told you I've had an accident."

He came through the doorway.

"Ah there you are! Sorry about your accident. Not much good for sales, are you?"

"We're closed really, only they left the door open for a customer who is coming to collect something."

He moved easily into the room and stood looking down at her. "As a matter of fact I've come to ask you to do me a favour."

"What is that?"

He grinned. "Quite in your line. I was at a sale the other day and picked up some odds and ends which might interest you. I thought of you at once. Perhaps you might like to dispose of them for me?"

Clover was interested. Of all things she loved the delicate side of the curio business: dainty ivories, little bits of china, filigree and the now fashionable necklaces, bracelets and rings of semi-precious stones, only a few of which she had acquired.

"I'd love to see them. Have you got them with you?"

"Sure I have." He put the box he had been carrying down on the table by her side.

As he bent to open it, she said, "By the way, what on earth made Bette rush off without saying good-bye? We were disappointed."

"Oh Bette," he dismissed her lightly, "she got news from London. She was very excited and I drove her to Penvale to catch the train. Something about her mother."

"Oh, her mother must be back then," said Clover.

He nodded. "Something like that. I gather the wire *was* from her mother. Anyhow off she went. Just as well really, she'd have been bored stiff on the farm."

"But she was coming to us," objected Clover. "Oh well, I suppose mothers come first."

Clover watched his face but he was bending over the box. It was a large box of heavy japanned wood about twelve inches by eight, and deep.

"I hear that your airman had another accident," she pursued as he fitted a key into the lock.

"Oh, what's that?"

"But surely you know. The police want to question you."

"The police? But he went off yesterday with a friend, that's all I know. I was called away early this morning and haven't been back yet. What *is* all this?"

Clover told him briefly what she had heard through the doctor. He listened, his face expressionless, then shrugged.

"Thought the chap was a bit touched—after all, you can't crash like that and get away with it. But how he got in the quarry is a mystery. At least it wasn't my responsibility."

He sounded casual and quite untroubled, entirely callous. By this time he had opened the box.

"How do you like the look of these?"

Clover leaned forward. The box was deep and lined with satin, and in it were what Nicholas called a collection of odds and ends. There were some old cameo brooches and rings, a necklace of amber and one of turquoise, wide barbaric-looking bracelets and one or two delicately chased silver spoons.

She took out one or two of the articles excitedly. "What a lovely lot of things! I shall have fun cleaning them and putting them up for display."

"They're yours—a job lot I picked up."

"How much do you want for them?"

He hesitated, then laughed. "All right, if you want to be business-like make it a quid. Only remember I want the box back."

Her bag was near at hand and she took out a treasury note. "I'm sure it isn't half enough. Thank you, Nicholas."

He waited, fingering the pound.

"I thought you were business-like—what about a receipt? Got any paper?"

She indicated a little pile of their own printed paper at the end of the table and he handed her a piece.

"What shall I put?" she asked. "Received of Nicholas Ferndale, various objects for one pound. Shall I list them?"

She spoke lightly, thinking that he was teasing her about her business methods, that was the kind of thing the old Nicky would have done.

"Something like that if you like." He had turned away as though he had lost interest, and, when she gave him the note, he put it in his pocket without glancing at it.

"Well, I must get on. As a rule I can leave the farm with the men, but things seem to have been happening since I drove away this morning."

He gave her a mock salute, ignored her thanks and walked lightly out of the shop, leaving Clover to turn over the contents of the box with new interest.

It had been decent of him to bring them in, and his byplay with the receipt had been reminiscent of the old Nicky. Really he had been charming. Probably Hugh and Tim were chasing a mare's-nest. At least she knew now that Bette was safe in London with her mother and new father as he had said, and as for the injured pilot, poor fellow, that mystery was a problem for the police.

She took up the amber necklace and let it fall through her fingers. She had always wanted a real amber necklace and had a mind to keep it for herself.

And so, as Hugh and Tim rode towards Grange Farm, their minds full of plots and counter-plots, Clover sat and examined the contents of the box Nicholas had so kindly brought round to her.

CHAPTER EIGHT

NEWS OF BETTE

HUGH and Tim cycled along the winding country road towards Grange Farm in thoughtful silence. Sometimes Tim whistled, or, with his usual interest in country things, asked Hugh the name of a bird he noticed in the hedgerow.

As they neared the farm Hugh said, "I thought you were going to ring up that man in London."

"I'd rather have a look-see round the farm first. May have something further to report, and he may be out until late. I'll ring his flat when we come back."

They approached the farm by its avenue of elms. Tim appraised it and made one comment.

"Decent little joint." His dark eyes were bright and interested.

They cycled down the drive and put their machines against some bushes. Hugh led the way to the door which was shut. He knocked loudly.

Mrs. Della appeared with such alacrity that Hugh suspected that she had seen them coming.

She gave him a look which held no liking.

"Oh it's you, is it? Boss is out, don't know when he'll be back."

"That's all right. I came to see Bette Danvers, my cousin. She's staying here, isn't she?"

"She's gone. Went this morning."

"This morning? Are you sure?"

The woman's eyes gave nothing away. "How should I know? I'm busy, see? Anyhow she isn't here."

"Know where she went?"

"No, I don't. Sorry I can't ask you in, but I'm busy getting the men's suppers. As if it wasn't bad enough usually, now there's all this fuss with the Air Force messing around and the police asking questions. I've had enough of it, I can tell you."

She seemed to be talking herself into a rage as she closed the door on them.

Hugh joined Tim and they began to stroll round the garden to the back.

"What do you make of it?" Hugh asked.

"That she wasn't sure of herself. She hadn't been primed with what to say. Perhaps the Boss, as she calls him, is really away."

"But surely she would have known if Nicholas had driven Bette to Penvale?"

Tim grunted. "I've told you my opinion. I don't think Bette *was* driven to Penvale."

No one seemed to be at the back. Beyond the paddock a big haystack had been raised and was already partly thatched, but the thatcher had long since left and there was no one in the outhouses or about the big barn; only a few hens picked in the straw ignoring a gaggle of geese which made the evening silence noisy with their shrill cackling.

Hugh made for the back door and quite boldly opened it. The long flagged passage ran through to the front of the house.

"Come on," he said to Tim.

Luckily they were both wearing shoes with rubber soles and moved along the passage silently. Hugh stopped by a hatch which gave, he knew, on to the big kitchen. It was like a window with dully paned glass. He caught Tim's arm. The murmur of men's voices reached them—the labourers were all at supper, no doubt, being served by the irritable Mrs. Della.

Hugh turned away and ran up the narrow staircase, Tim at his heels. He made for the rooms at the front, opening the door of the oriel room which had been his Uncle's. There was shaving tackle, and there was a pair of rather gaudy-looking pyjamas flung across the bed—probably this room was occupied by Nicholas.

"Now where did Bette sleep?" he murmured.

He opened the door beyond, but there was no sign that the room had been occupied by anyone. He was about to go out again when his sharp eyes noticed something on the trinket tray on the dressing-table.

It was a gold locket and chain and it belonged to Bette. He had seen it round her neck only the other day. He picked it up and put it in his pocket.

"Bette's?" asked Tim.

Hugh nodded. "This must have been her room. But why did she leave her precious locket? She always wore it."

Once on the landing again they continued their search. The rooms on the left side of the house were obviously taken over by the men who worked for the farm; some rooms contained two beds and a varied array of rough clothes, and shaving tackle.

The two boys were about to descend when they heard a stir below. The men had finished their supper and were returning to their work, the final work of a farm when beasts and fowls are closed up for the night.

"Let's go," said Hugh.

"How big is this farm?" asked Tim.

"About two hundred acres."

"I wonder how many men he has to work it?"

"Eight or nine, more than enough. Anyhow he sent off all the old hands when he returned and brought in his own lot."

"He would, of course."

They had reached the top of the stairs and were going down when the front door was flung wide and a tall figure stood there, back to the light.

"This is an unexpected pleasure," came the suave tones of the man Hugh knew as his cousin.

Hugh's homely face could look very stupid. He grinned. "Just blew in to show my friend round," he said, "this is Tim Benson, who is giving us a hand whilst Clover is laid up."

"Indeed, and very nice too. Have you had any food?"

"No, Mrs. Della was busy enough. Just stopped for a wash and now we're on our way again. By the way, we were sorry to miss Bette."

They stood in the hall now and the tall man stroked his beard. "Ah Bette. Well, perhaps I didn't make her as welcome as she expected and she was glad to go off to her mother."

"She went by Penvale, didn't she?"

The man shrugged: "I certainly left her there," he said ambiguously. "Well, what about some food? I'll hunt up that housekeeper of mine."

"Please don't trouble—we must be getting back," Hugh told him.

They went to get their bicycles. Everywhere the normal activities of a farm in the evening were going on. A man was driving some cows along the lower field, another hurried round with a bucket of pig food without a glance in their direction, whilst the thatcher was finishing off his work on the stack before dusk fell.

They turned left to the Penvale road which lay some five miles away.

"What's the idea of going to Penvale?" asked Tim.

"The station is small and the ticket collector may remember Bette if I describe her," Hugh answered.

The streets of Penvale wound down from a hill topped by the spire of its famous old church and at the foot of this hill lay the station which was an attractive little place with a brilliant garden.

The ticket-collector who was also the station master, no doubt, was a friendly, talkative fellow but, when Hugh asked him about a young girl travelling to catch the main-line train for London that morning, he pushed back his cap and ruffled his hair with a big hand.

"A gel, fair with curly hair cut short, come in a posh car? No, can't say as I saw any such person. Few people goes to Lunnon from 'ere as it means changing at Fairham. No one's booked for Lunnon to-day, I'll swear."

Hugh thanked him, and they walked with their bicycles across to a bus stop. Near there was a little square which had seats under three large plane trees. They both looked grave.

"Let's have a seat," said Tim. Hugh was inclined to forget that Tim was not strong for he was so energetic.

"Of course, let's. Have some chocolate and we'll buy some lemonade from that shop later." They put their machines against a tree and sat munching chocolate.

For the time neither of them discussed the news they had just heard—there was really nothing to discuss. They scarcely noticed a little old lady who had just sat down on the end of the bench they occupied. She carried a laden shopping basket and was obviously waiting for a bus.

At last Hugh spoke.

"I don't know what we shall tell Clover. You see what it means? Bette has not gone to London. Nicholas was lying. That wire too; it looks as though he sent it."

"I felt it in my bones," said Tim: "and I can't say I cottoned on to your Nicholas. There's a call-box over there. Do you think I should phone J. B. now? It's nearly seven."

"Easier from home," Hugh said, counting his

change. A trunk call from a call-box always worried him.

"Excuse me," said a high little voice, "I am afraid I could not fail to hear what you were discussing. You mentioned a girl called Bette and another name—Nicholas. Are you referring to a young girl called Bette Danvers?"

They both stared at the old lady sitting so primly there, searching their faces with an anxious, almost pleading, expression.

"Yes," said Hugh, "She's my cousin. We thought she had gone to London but have just found out that she can't have done so after all."

"Was she staying at the Grange Farm?"

Hugh nodded. "What do you know about her?"

The old lady looked most distressed. "Oh dear, and I didn't believe her. Not a word. She was so excited and I thought she was feverish, for she had certainly been in the forest all night."

Hugh put his arm on the frail arm. "You saw her—spoke to her? When?"

Miss Benham, for it was she, spoke tremulously. "Yes, but she would rush off, and I let her go. Now I realise that I was most unsympathetic. I shall never forgive myself."

Tim broke in, "Now, miss, don't get all het up. I'm sure you were very kind, but if you could tell us when you met her and all that it would help."

Miss Benham crossed her neatly gloved hands as though taking a hold on herself.

"Let me see, it was at about six this morning. Very early, but I get up then because of the animals. I found her by the fence in a fainting condition. My little house is on the verge of the forest and she had been wandering about all night—it was lucky she found me. I took her in and gave her some food and mended her clothes, poor child, but I could see she was not herself, though I put it down to her ordeal. She told me a most extraordinary tale." She paused. "Let me see, yes, something about staying at Grange Farm and a man who wasn't her cousin after all. Yes, and she talked of an aviator who had been thrown—*thrown!*—into the quarry and was lying there injured. Such a story. I felt sure she was rambling, then, when she saw I did not believe her, she rushed off."

The two boys listened with mixed feelings.

"Where do you live?" asked Hugh.

"Bracken Cottage. It is about half a mile down the lane from the Penvale road, very much off the beaten track. She seemed determined to get away; if she reached the main road she may have got a lift." She broke off. "I remember now—such a story. They set a dog on her and she climbed a tree. It all seemed too incredible here in dear England. What are the police doing," she went on in growing indignation, "to permit such things? If only I had not let her go."

Hugh managed a smile. "Knowing Bette, if she wanted to go she would. You couldn't have prevented her."

"I suppose not." She stood up. "My bus is coming. Now, if it is at all possible do let me know what happens. Miss Benham, Bracken Cottage off the Penvale Road. You should tell the police, you should really do that."

They handed her into the bus, a very worried old lady, then turned away.

Tim was half-way across the road. "I'm going to ring up J. B.," he called over his shoulder. "I've got change and I know these things. We can't tackle this alone."

He seemed to be in the call-box quite a long time before he finally came out.

"No luck, only got his manservant. But Bette must have rung last night. He said someone, a girl, had rung up with news about the accident to Ian Trent. He passed it on to J. B. when he returned this morning. Now J.B.'s gone out and he doesn't know where he is."

"He may have taken the matter up," said Hugh.

Tim looked depressed. "I don't know—in his own way he's important and he may have thought it was only a gag."

"Let's get back," said Hugh. He was thinking of Clover alone at home and, after what they had heard about Bette, he felt afraid even for her.

As they cycled out of Penvale they discussed the old lady's story from all its aspects. It seemed certain that Bette had found out a great deal too much for her own safety, that she had taken refuge in the forest and even been hunted. The fact that she had been free and well, if shaken, that morning was small comfort in the face of her disappearance now.

As they neared the Grange Farm again, Hugh looked thunderous.

"I'm going to see that man," he said.

"Hold hard, he's got a small body-guard, remember. We'd much better leave it to the police. We ought to get home to Clover."

Hugh stared at the cosy-looking farm desperately, although he knew that Tim was right.

They had passed the drive when they saw a large black Jaguar standing there. Its driver was just about to get in when Tim braked and nearly fell off his bicycle.

Without saying a word to Hugh he hurried up to the man who was about to start his car.

"I say, sir, I say!"

Hugh had an impression of a pleasant, ugly face, a big nose, rough greying hair and a pair of grey, very intelligent eyes, which now appraised them both, and especially Tim, in some amusement.

"Anything wrong, son?"

Tim almost stuttered. "I know you, sir, they call you J. B. at the office. I'm glad you've come, sir, just been trying to get you."

"Indeed. I've been paying a call, but I appear to have missed the person I wanted to see." The words sounded final—almost a snub.

"But didn't you get the message about the airman, sir?"

"I certainly got a somewhat garbled message, yes. What have you to do with all this?" The eyes showed amusement. "I do get odd messages now and then, you know."

Hugh broke in. "Are you really J. B. Smith, sir?"

"At your service." It was Hugh's turn to come under that shrewd scrutiny.

"Have you seen . . . er Mr. Ferndale?"

"I certainly have." The voice sounded somewhat grim.

"Well, Bette managed to get through to you, then she escaped but we don't know where she is now."

"Bette—do you mean Bette Danvers?"

"Yes, I'm her cousin, sir. We're awfully worried about her; you see she found out a lot about the pilot in the quarry."

"Wait!" The word was barked out. "Now, tell me, concisely if you can, exactly what you are talking about."

He sounded, Hugh reflected confusedly, a little like Field-Marshal Montgomery who had always been one of his heroes. As briefly as possible, Hugh told all he could; of Bette's arrival, her second visit, the plane crash and finally the wire. He told the man how they could find no trace of her until, by a chance which seemed like Providence, they had met Miss Benham.

J. B. listened. All the humour had left his face and he looked grim, very grim indeed.

When Hugh had come to a stop he nodded.

"Is that all?"

"I'd say it's enough, sir."

"I agree. Yes. Now, you go on home. Give me your address." Hugh did so and J. B. seemed to memorise it.

"Good. I've things to do, but I'll probably come in and see you later." He drew in the clutch, nodded to them unsmilingly, and drove off.

Hugh looked at Tim. "Is he always like that?"

"Don't ask me, I know him by sight, that's all. Still I'm glad he's on to it. We needn't worry now."

Hugh was not so sure. He had had the impression that J. B. Smith had been worried himself, very worried and very angry.

When they reached the shop it was dusk. The door was locked, so evidently the customer had come and gone. Hugh used his key and was absurdly relieved to see, beyond the darkness of the shop itself, light in the room at the end where Clover lay.

She greeted them with relief too.

"The man didn't come for his desk after all. But I managed to get up and lock the door." She laughed uneasily. "I know it is silly of me, but when it got dark I was a bit nervous."

They were very quiet.

"Well," she asked, "have you found anything out?"

Tim broke in hastily. "I must tidy up. J. B. will be coming."

Clover stared. "That Smith man you're always talking about?"

"Yes, we saw him by the farm." Tim was rushing round the room shaking cushions, adjusting books, tidying the table. "May be here any time. You tell her everything. Hugh, I haven't time. Besides you talk better than me."

Hugh had difficulty in starting: then he said: "Bette hasn't gone to London. We saw Nicholas who said she had, but the ticket-collector never saw her at Penvale. Then we had a stroke of luck." He went on to tell Clover about old Miss Benham and the story she had told them.

Clover listened in growing horror.

"Lost in the forest and they chased her with dogs! And she knew about Ian Trent being in the quarry, so it was she who rang up this morning and told the police."

"I don't know," frowned Hugh, "didn't the doctor say it was a boy's voice?"

"It must have been Bette."

"Then where is she now?"

Hugh brought out the locket. "I found this in her room at the farm—she always wore it."

"Oh well, she might have dressed hurriedly to go out. Yes, she must have found out something about Ian Trent which led to the quarry, and gone out. Then it was she who rang up Mr. Smith."

"Yes, must have been, but was it she who again rang the police this morning?"

Tim came in and flung a cloth on the table.

"Mind if I open the tin of salmon in the larder, Clover?"

"Poor Tim, you must be so hungry. Yes do, there's lettuce and tomatoes for a salad," said Clover mechanically.

Brother and sister watched Tim, their thoughts far away. Then Clover said: "By the way, he came to see me when you had gone."

"Who?"

"Nicholas."

"What did he want?"

She indicated the box. "Some lovely stuff in that box, though he wants it back—the box I mean."

Hugh opened it and examined the contents.

"Very nice, but what's the idea?"

"If it weren't for all this dreadful business, I'd say he was just being cousinly."

"Cousinly my foot! What's that Latin saying about distrusting the Greeks when they bring gifts?"

Tim came and peered at the contents of the box. He was about to say something when the bell rang.

"It's him," he said, "you go, Hugh."

Hugh strolled out with assumed calmness. He was rather in awe of J. B. Smith, and when he saw him looming over him at the door he was even more nonplussed. Their visitor was even taller than Hugh had guessed. However, Mr. Smith did not now look so grim. He wore no hat and was smoking a homely-looking pipe. Behind him, Hugh could see the large sleek car.

"Ah, there you are," he said, stepping in.

"You found us all right, then, sir," offered Hugh.

"My memory in unimpaired," said the other, with a grin.

Hugh led the way and introduced him to Clover. She was not shy, and liked the visitor on sight.

"Tim has told us a lot about you," she said.

"How did my name crop up then?"

"The pilot who crashed at Grange Farm gave Bette your name and telephone number," explained Clover. She added: "In case you haven't had time to have a meal we were hoping you'd take something with us."

"Delighted. Suppose we eat, then talk afterwards," said Mr. Smith easily.

Over the meal he refused to discuss serious matters although he seemed interested in their relationship to Bette.

"So she came to visit this other cousin of yours unexpectedly," he remarked.

"Yes, I felt she might not be welcome but she would go. Then she stayed on because of the accident."

"I see."

They ate, Mr. Smith had a word of praise for Tim's quite excellent coffee, then, when the meal was cleared away, he sat by the window and lit his pipe.

"Now, suppose we begin at the beginning. So far I know—that Bette arrived, saw you, went on to the farm and was not welcome. Ian Trent came down in his plane and she stayed that night. When did you see her again?"

"Yesterday afternoon," said Clover, "It was then that she told us all about the accident, and how Ian Trent had asked her to help him to get away. Bette thought that he was delirious, but, when Dr. Burton came and said that he was quite normal, I couldn't help feeling worried." She looked at Hugh who took up the story. He told of their visit to the farm, their encounter with the man who called himself Nicholas Ferndale and their journey to Penvale. When he got to their talk with Miss Benham, his listener stopped him to ask a few pertinent questions.

"At what time did she say Bette arrived?"

"Early, about six."

"And she'd been in the forest all night?"

"Yes, apparently. She was in rather a bad state, almost fainting. The old lady gave her food and mended her clothes."

"So now we've got Bette's story—although at third-hand only. She mentioned the injured pilot and said he was in the quarry?"

"Yes, and that she'd been tracked by dogs and had climbed a tree. It did sound quite mad really."

"And having given this information, finding the old lady incredulous—I must say with some reason—she hurried off," went on Mr. Smith. "It must have been she who rang up Jeavons last night—that would be before all this happened. Was it she who warned the police about a man in the quarry?"

"Well, the call came from the village near the Grange Farm and was said to be a boy's voice."

Their visitor puffed at his pipe. "It comes to this; we have lost all trace of her since her interview with Miss Benham early this morning. From there we must start." Quite abruptly he stood up, thanked Clover for the meal, nodded to the boys and said, as he moved down the shop: "Now, I want you to go on as though nothing had happened. If you see this cousin of yours be friendly, show no suspicion, and on no account mention me. I interviewed him to-day as a friend of young Trent. He gave nothing away. He told me what he has told the police—that Trent left in a car with a friend who called for him. He acted as though he had nothing to be afraid of, but I'm not so sure."

"Oughtn't we to go to the police?" said Hugh. "It's Bette, sir, it's the awful feeling that something may have happened to her, for she did know too much."

"I know." Mr. Smith put his hand on the boy's shoulder. "But I'll take care of everything. I am in touch with the police and, believe me, I shall do all I can."

"Will you try and see Ian Trent?"

"I rang the Infirmary before I came here. He will recover, but is still far too ill to give any account of himself."

They watched him drive off in his car, then closed the door.

"Don't worry, Hugh," said Tim. "We *can* leave it to him, you know."

CHAPTER NINE

THE LACQUERED BOX

As the two boys came back, Clover said, almost defiantly, "I liked him."

"Liked him!" Tim sounded scornful. "He's one of the cleverest lawyers in town, and when it comes to crime, he's got all it takes."

"If anything can be done, he'll do it," was Hugh's comment.

"If only we knew what had happened to Bette," said Clover. "If her mother knew she was missing, she'd be worried sick. I know Bette wrote to tell her she had come to the farm, but I suppose she's still away on holiday. It's just as well."

She looked very pale and, more to divert her from their unanswerable problems than anything else, Hugh pulled forward the lacquered box which Nicholas had brought in earlier that evening, and turned over the contents.

"Nice things. Let's go through them and you could clean them to-morrow, Clover. I wonder why he wants the box back?"

"It's a nice box, anyone might want to keep it," said Clover listlessly.

Hugh slowly emptied it, ranging the different pieces on the table, and then inspected the box. For its depth it was shallow, velvet-lined, with dusty corners.

Tim came forward eagerly. "Let's have a glim!" He peered inside it, closed it and examined it from ll sides.

"Eight inches deep outside, four inside," he said, ooking somewhat like a terrier at a rat hole, "wonder f it's got a false bottom."

He began to run his hands over the carvings round he sides—a design of Chinese dragons and lotus lowers. His thin hands paused, then he turned. "Got t!"

In pressing an unsuspected knob under the keyhole e had found the hidden spring. Something happened n the interior of the box: the red velvet bottom aised itself, disclosing a cavity a good four inches leep.

"Thought it was too shallow inside," Tim said.

They all stared at what lay in the box under the nnocent-seeming velvet bottom.

"Good lord," cried Hugh, "how on earth did they get there?"

For, packed neatly to the very rim were notes, five-pound and ten-pound notes—crisp and new as from the Bank of England.

Under Tim's fascinated eyes Hugh began to take them out and hand them to Clover who started to count them. In that apparently small space was over a thousand pounds in ten- and five-pound notes.

Tim, surprisingly, said nothing, but when they had taken all the notes out, he leaned forward and raised what still lay wedged beneath them—two plates such as printers use.

"Look," he said and held them to the light.

Each plate was etched with a replica of five- anc ten-pound note printing.

They all stared at them, fascinated.

"Do you see what this means?" cried Tim. "Forgery Why, I was reading that a lot of phony notes have beer passed here and on the continent. If only we'd founc this out before J. B. came."

Hugh took a five-pound note and held it to the light.

"The water mark's all right, as far as I know," he said. "Not that I'm particularly familiar with the water mark on bank notes!"

Clover made to stand up in her excitement, then fell back. Her foot was still unreliable.

"I've a couple of five-pound notes in the safe, Hugh, we didn't bank to-day. Get them."

Hugh went to the little safe which stood in a corner of the room and took out the money from the cash box. He held the notes to the light. Except that theirs were not so crisp and new, there was no difference and the water mark was identical.

Tim did the same in his turn.

"What do you make of it?" asked Clover.

The younger boy shook his head. "I don't know. These may be good notes, if not they are smashing forgeries."

"But why should Nicholas . . . that man, leave them with us?"

"As good a hiding place as any. Remember he's coming back for the box," said Hugh.

"He may have been afraid of the police searching the farm," said Tim.

"But he could have left the box at a bank."

"Remember to-day they close at twelve," Tim said.

"If only I'd mentioned the box to J. B.," said Clover, "I did say Nicholas had been, but I never thought to mention the box."

"If you had, what's the odds! We hadn't discovered what it held then." Hugh sighed. "I'm tired of all this mystery. Even if Nicholas isn't Nicholas, even if he's deep in a forgery game, it doesn't help us find Bette."

"I know." Clover lay back looking exhausted.

"It's past eleven; come, Timothy, let's hit the hay," suggested Hugh.

But, when the boys went up to their rooms Clover lay for a long time staring at the box, now closed and sitting innocently on the sideboard. What did it all mean? Nicholas had left it here with a purpose, but what?

The night seemed endless. When Clover at last heard the boys in the kitchen, the running of the tap, the pop of the gas and finally the hum of a kettle, she got up and limped out to wash. At least she could manage to get about a little now.

She tidied her settee, combed out her silky black hair and went to lie down again, and, soon after, Hugh arrived with her tea. She could hear Tim clattering in the kitchen.

"Had a good night?"

"No, did you?"

He grinned. "I always do. Well, it's Sunday."

"Do you think Mr. Smith will call in?"

"I don't know."

Tim came in with a tray. He looked very thoughtful. "I can't help wondering what is going on at the farm," he said. "It seemed all right, though those men looked like toughs. I'd like another glim to see how they spend their day of rest."

"On a farm, work goes on even on Sunday," commented Clover. "Hugh, ought we to tell the police about the box?"

Hugh shook his head. "Let's wait and see if J. B. turns up."

They were all restless and on edge that morning. It was Sunday and they missed the claims of the shop. Hugh went off to Church, for he was a member of the local choir. Clover insisted on limping about a little and helped cook the lunch with Tim's assistance; then they made her go out in the little garden and she began to occupy herself by cleaning the odds and ends of miscellaneous jewellery from the mysterious box

No one called, and the boys decided to take another ride.

"I thought we might go along the forest road and locate Miss Benham's cottage," said Hugh, "we might find some clues."

"Something to do at least," growled Tim, who was, for him, in a bad mood.

Clover understood their restlessness. "Yes, off you go."

"You will be all right?" Hugh suddenly sounded doubtful. "If anyone rings, I shouldn't answer."

"It might be Mr. Smith."

"I wish I knew where he was—he just breezed off. No, Clover, I shouldn't risk it. Or at least make sure who it is before you open the door."

"First show me your paws," she smiled.

"Something like that. There is certainly a wolf

about and I don't want you gobbled up like the seven little kids."

They left her in the little high-walled garden at the back of the house sitting under the acacia tree, the contents of the box on the small iron table, and the Sunday paper beside her.

When they had gone Clover polished away until the bracelets and rings and odds and ends glittered satisfactorily. Finally she read the paper: she read of the arrival of an important American diplomat, of a ship which had foundered in the North Sea, she admired the picture of her favourite film star and, yes, there was a mention that cleverly forged bank notes were still giving the police a good deal of trouble. She threw down the paper in disgust and the cat came and lay full length on it in the sun. Clover took up a book, then put it down. The door bell was ringing.

It was absurd but she felt nervous. Beyond the walls were other houses, but it was very quiet in the garden—everyone would have been tempted out on such a fine day. Still, she got up and, using her cane, limped into the house and through the shop.

The shop, with the blinds drawn, was a place of shadows, but the sunlight was full on the windows and, by the door, she saw a tall shadow, that of a man with an oddly pointed chin, a man with a beard. Clover stood very still, her heart beating quickly. It was Nicholas. Had he come for his box?

He rang again, waited, then moved away.

She had been afraid of him, yet he would scarcely have done her any harm—he had merely called for his box.

She returned to the garden again, annoyed with

herself and had scarcely settled herself in her chair when she heard the telephone ringing.

Again she got up and limped into the house.

The voice at the other end was suave and pleasant.

"Hullo, that's Clover, isn't it?"

"Yes."

"I called round ten minutes ago. Were you asleep?"

"No, I was in the garden."

"How d'you like your odds and ends?"

"Very much."

"Well, I'll be calling back at about six for the box so have it ready for me. That O.K.?"

"Of course, Nicholas, we'll have it ready."

She put down the receiver with a feeling of reprieve. The boys would soon be back.

They seemed a long time but it was well before six when they did arrive, both looking rather flushed and hot.

"Any news?" she asked.

"Anyone call?" asked Hugh.

"Nicholas did. He rang the bell twice but I didn't open the door. I just *couldn't*, Hugh—funny, but I felt quite frightened. Then he telephoned to say he'd be round at about six."

"We shouldn't have left you."

"Nonsense. Anyhow he wants the box—what shall we do?"

They were all silent.

"I know," said Tim, "take out the notes et cetera, and give it to him empty, he won't know."

"He might look," said Clover.

Hugh glanced at his watch. "Only half-past five—I'm making some tea."

"But what did you do? Did you see the old lady?"

"Yes," Tim grinned. "Hugh, you're a food hound! We had a lavish tea there, scones and jam and home-made cake."

"She's got some beautiful dogs and is giving us a spaniel pup when it's old enough to leave its mother," added Hugh.

"Anything more about Bette?" asked Clover.

Hugh had the grace to look rebuked. "No, she blames herself, poor old thing, for not believing her, but though we questioned her, she couldn't tell us anything more."

"She's been missing now since early yesterday morning." Clover looked from one to the other in new distress. "And that man Smith doesn't seem to have done anything."

They were all looking soberly at each other when they heard the door bell ring again.

"Nicholas," said Clover.

"You go, Hugh, I'll empty the box," said Tim.

Hugh tried to laugh. "Well don't look so scared, Clo, there are three of us."

He strode in and through the shop. The figure outside was not Nicholas, it wore a peaked cap and what appeared to be uniform. Hugh unhooked the door to find himself facing Inspector Skelton, a pleasant red-faced man who had known Hugh since the old Grange Farm days.

"Good evening, son," he said, "could I have a word with you and your sister?"

"Of course, come in, Inspector."

Once in the dimness of the shop Hugh looked at the other's candid face.

"It's about our cousin, isn't it? I . . . you haven't any news yet?"

"Not yet, but I thought I'd like a word with you first-hand as it were. Funny business altogether."

At least no news was good news. Hugh led the way through the sitting-room, where Tim and been busy doing something to the box. When he saw the uniform he half-turned, concealing it. He looked, Hugh noticed, absurdly guilty.

Inspector Skelton greeted Clover genially then sat and began to ask questions. They all rather gathered from the trend of them that he had already talked to J. B. Smith. Painstakingly he went over old ground: when had they last seen Bette, what had she told them, about the farm, about the air crash, about the pilot. He heard the story of her night's experiences without comment and, having come to the end of the interview, was about to leave when Clover exchanged glances with her brother.

"There's something else," said Hugh.

"Something else?" The Inspector waited.

Clover took up the story. "Yesterday, Nicholas—Mr. Ferndale—brought me a box with some odds and ends in it to sell," she indicated the things on the table. "Last night we found the box had a false bottom. Inside, under the velvet, were a lot of notes."

The Inspector looked puzzled. "Notes?"

"Bring the box and the notes out, Tim," ordered Hugh.

The Inspector had not seemed particularly interested, but when he saw the notes and the plates he picked them up, held them to the light and then turned on them sharply.

"You say your cousin brought these concealed in the box?"

"Yes," said Clover. "He told me to take the contents and let him have the box back, but Tim found a spring and . . . and we found the notes."

"You say that Mr. Ferndale brought these?" The Inspector was frankly incredulous.

"Yes, and he's coming back for them at any moment now."

Inspector Skelton began to put the notes and plates methodically back into their hiding place. "I shall have to take these with me. This is very important," he said.

They were all silent. It was hot in the little garden and they all felt that their little story, their find, had alienated them from their visitor. Hugh was about to speak when the distant buzz of the bell sounded again.

"That will be Nicholas," he said, "I'll go and let him in."

"And you'll be able to question him yourself," added Clover.

Hugh hurried away; the visitor was Nicholas all right. He stood fanning himself with his slouch hat. His car lay behind him at the kerb.

"Ah, someone is in this time."

"Come in," said Hugh. "Jolly glad you have come as a matter of fact. We're all in the garden."

Nicholas strolled nonchalantly behind him, then paused in the doorway when he saw the uniformed figure on the lawn.

"It's Inspector Skelton—he came to ask us about Bette, she's missing." Hugh watched the dark face.

"Then we told him about the box. It's a good thing you've come in time to explain."

Nicholas raised his dark brows. "The box—what box?" he asked lightly, then he walked across the grass.

"Good evening, Inspector, didn't know you worked on a Sunday, thought you left it to us poor farmer chaps."

"Good evening, sir. I'm glad you've arrived. You may be able to clear up a certain matter." He indicated the box and the pile of notes. "Miss Ferndale here tells me that you brought this box to her here last night. It contained semi-precious jewellery but has a false bottom. Can you explain the presence of these notes and the plates, sir?"

Nicholas laughed quite easily. "I'm afraid not. I never saw either box or contents in my life before—my cousin must be suffering from delusions."

"Are you quite sure, sir? The young lady definitely told me that you brought the box last night."

"I gave him a receipt for it," added Clover, her voice high and strained.

Nicholas shrugged. "You see, Inspector."

"But, Nicholas, you did, you even rang more than an hour ago to say you were coming to collect it!"

Nicholas looked at her in well-assumed bewilderment.

"Now, now, Clover, my dear, why tell such a naughty little fib? Now take my advice and come clean. It doesn't do to try and fool the police."

Tim interfered for the first time. He came forward, his thin face flushed.

"See here, whoever you are, we know a bit about

you. It's you who are the liar, and worse. What about Ian Trent, and yes, what about Bette?" He turned to the Inspector. "Just you ask him that, sir, just you do. Ask J. B. Smith what he knows."

Inspector Skelton was obviously out of his depth. He stared from the white-faced girl to Hugh, who was not white but red and incoherent with anger. He was about to speak when the man Nicholas smiled.

"You little whipper-snapper, there's a law for slander, you know!"

Tim clenched his fists, but Hugh got in front of him.

"It's no good, Tim. We know he's a liar, we know he brought this stuff here for his own reasons." He looked at the Inspector almost pleadingly. "He *is* lying, you know. He did come last night and leave this box. It was only a chance that led us to find the notes. It's his word against my sister's. You'll have to make up your mind about that."

The Inspector was still manifestly ill-at-ease.

"You abide by your statement, Miss Clover, that Mr. Ferndale left this box here last night, and that you had no idea of the concealed contents?"

"Yes," Clover spoke bitingly, the glance she gave Nicholas held hate. "And," she added, "you'd better get a search warrant for Grange Farm. Our cousin Bette has disappeared, as you know. It was he who said she had gone to London and that he drove her to Penvale. We know she hasn't."

"Leave that for the present," barked the Inspector. "What concerns me now is this box. I shall take it with me and communicate with London at once. If, as I think, these notes are forged, I'm afraid you will have to do a lot of explaining."

Nicholas smiled disarmingly at Clover.

"Now, my dear, why all this mystery? The box was found in your possession—how did you come by it? It isn't a bit of use trying to blacken my name. Inspector Skelton remembers me when I was here, and Dad was alive, I've no reason to take to—forgery is it? Neither have I any reason to prevent Bette from returning to her mother. Be sensible now, I should. Tell him everything and you'll save yourself a lot of trouble, eh, Inspector?"

"Sounds sensible advice to me, sir," said the Inspector. "If she tells us where she got the stuff a more lenient view would be taken."

Hugh broke in. "Look here, there is something very queer going on at the farm. We traced Bette—he even set dogs on her!"

Nicholas laughed. The Inspector shook his head.

"Now, Mister Hugh, I'd be careful what you say, it doesn't do to trifle with the law."

Tim stepped forward. "Ask him how that airman got in the quarry."

Nicholas met the Inspector's glance.

"It's incredible, isn't it, Inspector? Never mind, I'll go bail for them if the worst comes to the worst—after all, they're little more than kids."

The Inspector was writing at the table and did not answer. "A receipt for the box and contents, Miss Clover. I must go now and communicate with Scotland Yard. I'll be back of course."

Nicholas turned away. "I must be getting along. I can run you wherever you want, Inspector."

Skelton nodded. "Thank you, sir. I'd like a little talk with you in private."

He turned to the three young people. "Now, when I come back, just be ready to tell me what it's all about. It doesn't do to conceal things from the police." He sounded a little less grim. He turned away, and followed Nicholas out through the shop.

They heard the sound of the high-powered car as it raced away down the narrow street.

CHAPTER TEN

UNDER SUSPICION!

FOR an appreciable moment after they were alone all three remained speechless. It was Tim who found his voice first.

"For crying out loud! Of all the sheer bald-faced cheek! You see, he's got us in wrong with the police on purpose, so that they won't listen to us."

Hugh nodded. "I think I do see."

Clover was near to tears. "It was dreadful—trying to make the Inspector think I was lying. As though I would. Hugh, it means our business will be ruined. Suppose I can't prove how I got that box?"

"Nonsense, Sis. He can't get away with it like that, and the police aren't fools. We know something odd is going on at the farm and . . ." he broke off, "I wonder what's happened to J. B.; surely he'll believe us."

Tim brightened. "Crikey, yes, he'll cook that fellow's goose."

"Well, where is he then?" asked Clover indignantly. "And Bette, don't forget she's still missing."

A low rustle reached them from the leaves.

"It's raining," she added, then began to laugh a little hysterically. It was raining, suddenly and very hard. In the stress of the last hour they had not noticed the gathering clouds or even the distant rumble of thunder. Now, abruptly, the storm was upon them. Hugh helped his sister into the house, and Tim gathered up books and papers only just in time. Inside it was shadowy and, within ten minutes, Fairham was experiencing one of those sharp summer storms which make minor headlines in the papers. Thunder roared, lightning played, and Clover at least felt that the turmoil fitted in with her mood.

Tim prepared a meal which they took in sober silence. After the meal the storm, though not the rain, which still fell in torrents, abated. Hugh sat at the table and took pencil and paper.

"What are you doing?" asked Clover.

"Getting down the facts, making a memorandum to show that wooden-headed Inspector."

Tim came and looked over his shoulder. "Mind you get everything in!" Clover took up her crochet but her hands felt shaky, though whether from the effects of the storm or that interview in the garden, she did not know. She watched the boys as they consulted over the various notes. For half an hour they worked, then Tim nodded. "That should do."

"Let me see."

Hugh handed over four pages covered by his neat handwriting.

It was headed *For the attention of the Police.*

1. Return of (alleged) Nicholas Ferndale last year.
   (a) Old hands paid off.
   (b) Strangers installed—"toughs".
   (c) Money gift from N. F. to Clover and Hugh Ferndale.
2. Arrival of Bette Danvers.
   (a) Unwelcome but induced to stay after crash.
   (b) Trent recognises N. F. as someone called Smiler. Asks Bette to help him get away.
   (c) Trent discovered, injured, in quarry.
   (d) Bette disappears. N. F. says she has gone to London. This proved untrue.
   (e) Miss Benham's story. Bette lost in forest Friday night. N. F. tried to capture her. She rang up J. B. on Friday night. No trace of her after she left Miss B.
3. Saturday and Sunday.
   (a) Police get message (boy's voice?) about man in quarry. Ian Trent found.
   (b) Hugh and Tim at farm. Find Bette's locket. Meet J. B. who has been to see N. F.
   (c) N. F. arrives with box. Later notes and plates are discovered.
   (d) N. F. phones to say he is coming for box. Arrives to find Inspector with us. Denies all knowledge of box and throws the can at Clover.

Finally, where is Bette? What is going on at the farm?

Is N. F. the real Nicholas?

Clover read it through. "I think," she said when

she had finished, "that it all hangs on the last question. If it isn't Nicholas but someone who is pretending to be he, both Ian Trent and Bette would be in danger. Certainly something strange is going on at the farm, but if he isn't Nicholas, I would think he'd be content to stay a prosperous farmer and not risk the police getting too interested in him."

Hugh frowned: "That's the point, if he isn't Nicholas, who is he? Don't you see though, that once Trent recovers—and he will recover, we have Smith's word for that—that will be cleared up."

"Yes," sighed Clover, "if he is an impostor it doesn't look as though he can get away with it for long now. But how did we take him so much for granted?"

"I guess we were gulled. We remembered a boy of sixteen and when he came back and was accepted by everyone, we never thought otherwise. And there is a resemblance in height and colouring, enough, at least, to take us in. It was like a sort of—of preconceived idea," he finished grandly and probably with truth.

"I'd say he's playing for time. He brought the box here because he was afraid the game was up and the Farm might be searched. Then he finds the Inspector and just acts himself out of it all and puts the guilt on us." Tim stopped then added, "If only J. B. would show his hand!"

"And meanwhile what about Bette?" asked Clover.

The two boys were silent. They all remembered what had happened to the airman. Bette knew a great deal; would the man who called himself Nicholas Ferndale have any mercy when it came to her?

It was late when they retired. Outside the rain still fell. Clover heard the patter of it on the leaves outside the window; that and her anxiety kept her awake.

Anxiety for Bette, and hate and fear of the man who had lied so blatantly, filled her thoughts. She, in possession of forged notes! Why, they could put her in prison for that! But when Ian Trent was better he would speak, and then there was J. B. Smith. Where was he? What had happened to Bette? If only Mr. Smith would come back, *he* would help. He had seemed kind and clever. She dozed, she slept and had a terrible dream.

She was in the long passage which led from the front to the back of Grange Farm. Both doors were closed and it was pitch dark. She could hear the beat and swish of rain outside and she knew that the moat would be filling. She could hear the water rushing and flooding all around her, then from the front door came a knocking. She stood unable to move, afraid of who waited there, then she heard herself saying. "Who is it?" "It's Bette, Bette, let me in," came the voice in her dream. She fought and struggled to open the door but she could not do so. She was still trying to force it open when she awoke, bathed in perspiration, to find the sun streaming into the room and Hugh standing over her with a cup of tea.

"Gosh, Sis, who were you fighting?"

She sat up. "I had an awful dream."

"Never mind now, drink this. It's only six o'clock, but I woke early. Tim's still hogging it, from the sounds."

He left her and she drank the tea and washed and dressed. It was Monday, after the longest week-end she remembered. To-day she would move about more, her foot was already much better. She would persuade

Hugh and Tim to go to the farm again whilst she saw to the shop. She remembered Inspector Skelton. He might come back—by this time he would have got in touch with his superiors and shown them the box and its hidden contents. Would she be arrested on suspicion? She tried to quell this new fear as she heard Tim whistling in the kitchen.

"I'll make the breakfast this morning," she told him.

"What's come over you? You should stay put for another few days, according to the doc."

"I don't intend to, so that's that."

"O.K. don't glare at me!"

She smiled; really it was too bad of her to be irritable, Tim had been very helpful. "I'm sorry, you're an angel, but I want you and Hugh to go over to the farm to-day and have another look round."

"That's O.K. by me. What worries me is what has become of J. B."

"Maybe he's lost interest, didn't believe us."

"Maybe my foot, he isn't like that. No, he's playing his own game."

They had finished breakfast by half past seven, and then Clover went round the shop with Tim, rearranging things in her own way. Thanks to him, trade had by no means fallen off. He showed her the little book in which he had kept careful account of sales and when Clover insisted on him taking commission they had quite an argument.

"But it's my holiday," he reiterated. "I never enjoyed myself so much in my life, selling things, and all this mystery into the bargain."

"And a visit from the police," added Clover grimly.

"Not so good, I agree. But not to worry, once that

Trent chap tells his tale it will be all up with Mr. Smiler Nicholas, see!"

"I wonder how he is; perhaps Doctor Burton will tell me when he comes. By the way, keep a sharp look-out for him. I don't want him ticking me off for disobeying orders."

"Well don't put yourself back," warned Hugh.

When the shop opened it was to quite a few customers. The little town had now its complement of visitors, many of them families who used the old town as a stopping place, driving daily from it to the sea. Children stopped to peep at Hugh's toys and, at ten, Tim hurried off on business of his own. He returned with a large, long, unwieldy bundle.

"What on earth?" cried Bette who sat in the shop polishing some old glass.

A bucket clattered to the floor followed by half a dozen more, and there was also about a score of spades and more buckets in the bulky parcel.

"For the kids. I wrote to a wholesale place in Stepney who sell 'em. Nice little profit on them, see the invoice."

"Oh Tim, but this isn't a toy-shop!"

"Left side is, and why not? You want to make money, what's the difference between a coral necklace or a bucket and spade?"

It was no use arguing, and before the morning was over, they had sold more than a dozen buckets and spades. Indeed they were so busy that the boys were unable to get away. Over lunch Clover persuaded them.

"Bette might still be there. Do go and have another look."

She was so insistent that they agreed, promising not to be away for longer than two hours. So they went off at one-thirty, but not before Tim warned her: "A gentleman, a real toff, grey, a bit screwy-looking is after the oak chest. And don't forget I asked ten pounds for it."

"I listed it at eight," protested Clover.

"Never mind, it's worth ten and he was nibbling on Saturday. And remember, green spades are one and ten, the red, two and six, and buckets all two and nine."

Clover smiled in spite of herself. She began to wonder who was managing the shop, she or he, but it was impossible not to appreciate his enthusiasm.

As soon as she was left alone Clover began to feel, if not nervous, wary. Until two-thirty scarcely anyone called, and alone, constantly glancing out at the street, she noticed something which had eluded her during the busy morning.

A big man in grey flannels was pacing up and down. He would pause to look at shop windows, or to light a cigarette, and for more than half an hour he stood in the doorway of the offices opposite, reading a paper. At first she thought he was waiting for someone, but when he continued to wait, she watched him with more interest. Then he took off his soft hat and wiped his forehead with a large white handkerchief and suddenly she recognised him. She had seen him often enough pacing the streets, but in policeman's uniform. He was one of the local police and he was here to watch her shop, because—because they were suspect.

She went cold at the thought and when a mother and her small boy came in to choose one of Hugh's animals, her manner was so vague that the customer looked at her sympathetically.

"Does your foot pain you badly?" she asked, as she paid for a kangaroo.

Clover had almost forgotten her bound foot.

"Oh no, it's getting better."

"I'm glad. Have you no one to help you?"

"Oh yes, but my brother is out at the moment."

The kindly woman left her full of admonitions.

The afternoon seemed endless—even the watcher had gone off, probably for refreshment. Customers came and went, and Tim's old gentleman, the one he had described as " a toff and a bit screwy " came in to examine the chest. He proved to be Colonel Bampton, a retired army officer and quite an old friend.

"That lad of yours said ten pounds, m'dear, but that's steep even nowadays," he commented.

Clover smiled. "As a matter of fact he has the idea that it's good business to put up prices. I'm asking eight."

"Ah, that's more in my line," he laughed. "Don't want to rob you though, my dear."

"No, really, Colonel, the price is eight."

He seemed satisfied and wrote her a cheque there and then. When he had gone, having made arrangements for delivery, Clover felt amused. Even though she had sold her chest at the original price, the right window had won against the left for once. "As though I could overcharge the dear old Colonel," she thought.

Some tourists came and looked round, a few children came, and she made a few more modest sales from the left window. Would the boys never return? She looked out of the window. The plain-clothes man was back again, pacing up and down and looking hot and bored. On impulse she waved to him. He turned and came in, looking slightly embarrassed.

"Yes, miss?"

"I only wanted to know if you'd like a cup of tea. I've just put the kettle on."

He flushed all over his honest face. "Very kind of you, I'm sure, miss. I could do with a cup."

"Good, it must be awfully tiring watching this place. Haven't we had a lot of customers?" she asked naughtily.

He grinned and took out his notebook: "Eight adults, eleven children this afternoon. This morning, let's see, one, two, three, four, adults, eleven children; I haven't counted the Colonel, knowing him."

"I say, did you have to make a note of everyone?"

"Not much use if I didn't take notes. Never trust to memory, that's my motto, miss. Always make notes, and very interesting and helpful they prove."

"Well, will you keep an eye on the shop whilst I make the tea? I shan't be five minutes," said Clover cheerfully.

In the end, having drunk his tea, he actually bought one of Hugh's jumping clowns. It had given Clover a wicked satisfaction to entertain him, though he continued to remain on the watch.

"Anyhow I needn't feel nervous with him around," she reflected, glancing at the old grandfather clock which was one of her treasures. Ten past five; Hugh and Tim had been away for more than three hours. When she heard the ringing of bicycle bells as they cycled round the corner she watched them arrive almost nervously. They looked hot and excited. Was there news then?

"What is it?" she asked.

"We don't know exactly, tell you in a minute." Hugh carried his machine through the shop, followed by Tim who gave a quick glance round.

"Sold the chest?"

She nodded: no need to tell him that she had asked the original price.

It was time to close the shop, so she left Tim to do this and went to get tea.

He was back a moment later though. "You spill the beans, Hugh, there's a dame hovering at the window. No good turning away custom because of overtime."

"Well," asked Clover, "What's the news?"

"We went to the farm."

"Yes, yes, any sign of Bette?"

"No, nothing I'm afraid but . . ."

"For goodness' sake, tell me, something queer has happened, I can see."

"I'll say it has." With various interruptions from his sister, Hugh told his story.

They had got to the farm in mid-afternoon and gone straight to the front door and rung. No one had come. It proved to be locked and when they went round to the back they soon discovered that the place was strangely deserted.

"It was the oddest experience, Clover," Hugh said. "That big place—you know how big it is—stables, barns, the oast house, the big yard, were all absolutely deserted. We tried the back door and it was closed and barred too. There were hens and geese about left to wander where they wanted. The cows, the fine Jersey herd, were in the field, though the horses had been brought in. We wandered through the fields and the haymaking machine stood in the middle of Low Meadow, half the grass cut, but untended with not a soul about."

"Do you mean to say that none of the men were seeing to things?"

"I told you, not a soul. Tim and I went back to the house and we managed to get in through the pantry window, at least Tim managed, and came and let me in. We had a thorough search of the place. On Saturday the men's rooms had been full of their belongings, now they were gone. Even the room occupied by Mrs. Della—we guessed it was hers from hairpins and an old net on the dressing-table—was empty; not a hairbrush, not a bit of soap, not a thing. His room, he had the oriel room, you know, was empty too. I tell you, the house is just an empty shell. You see what it means?"

"Of course, he's got away and his accomplices have dispersed. That must have been why he brought the box here, he was planning ahead. Now perhaps the police will believe that there is something wrong about Mr. Ferndale of Grange Farm." She broke off. "But we still don't know what has happened to Bette. Hugh, what shall we do?"

"Go to the police, of course. They are our only hope, now that J. B. seems to have let us down."

"You won't have to go far," Clover said, and told him about the friendly policeman who had been watching their shop all day. "I suppose there was no one watching the farm?" she added.

"Not a soul as far as we could tell. You know that it is off the beaten track along that narrow lane. I hung round until five and Tim went into the village to make inquiries. Result absolutely nil. Mrs. Brett the postmistress had seen Mr. Ferndale pass through in his car on Sunday, that was all. Since the farm has been run by strangers, few go that way; in fact there is a rather unpleasant feeling against my lord Ferndale for obvious reasons. He employs no local labour, the farm is practically self-supporting, and even the necessary stores come by rail from London! No, no one in the village knows a thing."

"Why did you stay so long then?"

Hugh grinned for the first time. "You should guess!"

"Waiting for someone to turn up?"

"A lot of use that would have been. No, the cows. I waited late to milk them. I left it all in the dairy and goodness knows whether anyone calls for it or who disposed of it. I suppose it was taken to Fairham—he must have had some contract with the Milk Marketing Board. But Clover, think of it, a farmer leaving a herd of cows just to wander in the field with no one to milk them—he ought to be shot! Anyhow I did it, even Tim tried to milk, but that's one thing he can't do."

"It's queer," said Clover, "I suppose you'll have to go back to-morrow to see to them."

"Of course. I think I'll get hold of old Selwyn, he'll help me in this crisis. Yes, that's a good idea."

"But perhaps they'll come back to-morrow."

"Do you really believe that? No, it's my idea that Nicholas, if we can call him that, has made a complete getaway, his gang are scattered and he's off to heaven knows where."

Tim appeared. "Made a sale and I've closed. Now for tea."

Clover looked at them helplessly. Nicholas might have gone never to return—that didn't worry her—but what had become of Bette?

CHAPTER ELEVEN

THE VISITOR

WITH Tim they discussed the evacuation of the farm in all its aspects; Tim himself had come to the obvious conclusion.

"Seems this man, who is no more your cousin than I am, has just bunked because things were getting too hot for him. As for Bette," he broke off, "I never thought J. B. would let us down like this."

"Perhaps he hasn't," said Clover, "he seemed so nice. Perhaps he's following up some clue."

Tim brightened. "That might be it, but I wish he'd turn up, at that."

Dr. Burton put in an appearance after his surgery, and, finding Clover no longer resting, had a few caustic things to say about her lack of care. However, the foot was getting on well and, as he bandaged it again, she asked him about Ian Trent.

"He'll be all right, he's lucid at last."

"Do you mean he can talk?" cried Hugh.

"Yes. The police were waiting at his bedside when he came to."

"Then they know!" cried Clover.

Dr. Burton would not be drawn. "Know what, young lady? You leave well alone, the police know their business."

Clover flushed. Had the news that their place was being watched got out? In this she much misjudged the police, as she was later to discover. Dr. Burton had certainly heard rumours but nothing more. At any rate he refused to discuss anything with them. Even when Hugh asked him if he knew that Grange Farm was deserted he showed neither interest nor surprise, merely cautioned Clover to go carefully with her foot, took up his bag and hurried off.

Hugh was restless that evening.

"I keep thinking of those animals with no one in the place. The horses are in their stables, fed and watered, the cows should be all right but I must ride over at daybreak and see to them."

"Once a farmer always a farmer," chided Clover, "they'll be all right."

"I suppose so, but I'm uneasy."

The evening crawled. Clover found herself glancing at the clock and they had not the heart to put on the radio. Tim got busy with accounts at his corner of the table, Hugh, after wandering in and out of the garden, began to work on the animals for the Noah's Ark he was doing. When, abruptly, the bell rang they all started and looked at each other.

"The police!" cried Clover, and went rather white.

Hugh went through the shop and Clover, unable to

stay where she was, snatched her stick and limped after him.

A tall shadow showed against the blind.

"Not police," muttered Hugh as he fumbled with the catch of the door.

He opened it, then stared aghast at the tall tanned man who stood there, for he was tall, tall as the false Nicholas. His dark eyes, alert and bright in his tanned face, were somehow familiar, as was the dark brown hair with a kink in it.

The stranger stood and smiled at them; a considering smile, half serious, half amused, then Clover gave a little scream, and, throwing herself forward, caught him by the arms as though to assure herself of his reality.

"Nicky! Nicky! Oh!" Then she began to sob. She had been through so much in the last few days that this was too much.

Nicky Ferndale, Nicky who could never be the Nicholas they had met in his place, held her hands gently. He looked concerned, almost abashed.

"Now, now, little Clover . . . it is, isn't it? And you'll be Hugh. By jove, you have grown up, you two. May I come in?"

He walked in and it was he who closed the door behind him. "I only arrived in England two days ago," he explained calmly. "Knew there was something funny up when I went to the farm and found it deserted. Folks in the village told me you were here so I came along. Saw old Selwyn, seemed to think I was a ghost, and, lord knows, I feel like one.'

Hugh found words at last. "Nicky, you don't know what it means to see you. We'd quite made up our minds you were dead. That chap said he was you, you know."

Nicky Ferndale gave him a sharp look. "He did, did he? Well, it isn't his fault that I'm *not* dead."

He stared round the sitting-room where Clover had mechanically led him. "Not a bad little place, this."

Tim was standing, staring.

"This is Tim," explained Clover vaguely—she still had the feeling that she was in a dream. "Tim, this is Nicky, the real Nicky."

Tim was equal even to this. "Glad to meet you, sir. Matter of fact I suspected all the time that the other chap was having us on."

Nicky sat down and stretched out his long legs.

"Now suppose you tell me what's been going on. I gather that this chap, 'Smiler' Garth, he's called, turned up with my papers and installed himself in my place." He looked at Hugh in whimsical reproach. "I know I've changed after all these years, and that there is a superficial likeness, but I'd hate to be taken for that fellow."

Hugh flushed. "I know, but it *is* years and what with the beard and everything and finding him there, kind of taking it all for granted. . . . Of course we thought you'd changed for the worse, but we put it down to all you had been through."

"I think I see. You accepted him. Now go on, tell me everything that happened."

Hugh, with interpolations from Clover, told him. How the man had claimed the farm, turned them and the old servants out, and brought in his own gang.

When they got to recent events Nicky got up and paced restlessly up and down.

"Bette—you mean little Bette Danvers—in his hands?"

"Yes, she came to stay at the farm. He was going to send her away, then there was this accident. The pilot recognised *him* and Bette must have found out something when she went back on Friday. *He* said she had returned to London, but she hasn't."

Hugh went on to tell of their encounter with Miss Benham, of the arrival of J. B., and about the box and its contents.

"And there is still no word of Bette?"

"No, we're frightened," said Clover.

"But what has been done? Have you told the police?"

"J. B. said he would." Clover felt hot. What *had* they done? Had they been horribly casual in their reaction to their cousin's disappearance?

"J. B.? I know nothing about what he is doing," Nicky was saying, when the door-bell rang again. Hugh went to answer it and they all waited in silence. They heard steps in the shop and the murmur of voices, then Hugh came in followed by a broad-set middle-aged man: it was J. B. Smith himself.

He appraised Nicky. "So you've come back. Hope my bit of wire-pulling helped. Name's Smith."

Nicky's face cleared. He held out his hand.

"By jove, sir, if it was you who confirmed my story and got the powers-that-be busy, I'm jolly grateful. It was tough arriving home without an identity."

Suddenly Clover realised that he had told them nothing of his own adventures; of how he and the man who had cast such a shadow over their lives had changed places.

"But what happened?" she asked.

"Look here, all in good time," J. B. smiled at her reassuringly, "I came over for the boys."

Clover put her hand on his arm. "What about Bette? You said you'd tell the police for us—she isn't back."

He smiled. "Now, will you believe me if I tell you that Bette is all right?"

Clover relaxed, something tight and frightened seemed to break in her. "Thank you," was all she managed.

J. B. was addressing the others again. "Now, you boys, you can be useful, and you, Ferndale, of course. It's about the farm."

What's happened?" cried Hugh.

"Just got the news—it's on fire."

Hugh flushed. "The animals—I closed them in!"

"Easy, easy, where are you going?" For Hugh was already half-way to the door.

"To the farm, of course."

Nicky spoke briskly. "Has a fire alarm gone out?"

"Of course. Meanwhile we shall want all the helpers we can get. I've my car outside. You'd all better pack in."

Nicky faced him. "Is it very bad?"

"I don't know, but the sooner we get there the better. The fire engine is on its way, and, after the storm yesterday, there should be enough water in the pond and moat."

They were going, forgetting her. Clover felt she

could not wait here alone. She limped forward to Nicky.

"Nicky, I'm coming, I must."

He smiled. "All right, Clover. Room for her in the car, sir?"

Smith nodded. "We'll make it, but mind that foot of yours, young woman, and remember you can't do much to help."

"I know, but I just couldn't wait alone."

The older man had walked ahead.

"He says Bette is all right. Hugh, are you sure she wasn't there at the farm?"

"We searched the place, I told you."

Nicky turned. "Did you search the vaults?"

"No. No, they were locked."

"Come on, let's get going," said Nicky.

J. B. was waiting for them by his car. Clover had to be sure.

"About Bette. You're sure she isn't there—that she's all right?"

"I give you my word, now into the back of the car. Careful!" He gave her an odd little smile. "What do you think I've been doing the last two days?"

"You mean you've seen Bette?"

He only smiled.

"Is that so, sir?" asked Nicky.

"Never commit myself unless I'm sure. Bette's all right. Now pack in quickly."

His car was a roomy one. It was the Jaguar the boys had first seen him in and it easily accommodated them all: Clover and Hugh at the back, Tim wedged in by Nicky and Mr. Smith.

With a roar of released engines it turned up Fore

Street and away into the country. Dusk had fallen now, and soon, as they took the rise which led to the farm, they saw a weaving glow in the sky. Hugh muttered to himself.

"Why did I shut the animals in? If only I'd had the sense to leave them free!"

"The first thing the firemen will do is let them out," Clover reassured him. In spite of what lay before them a great weight had lifted from her: Bette was safe—she had J. B.'s word for that, and Nicky, the real Nicky, was back. She felt almost happy, in spite of that sinister glow.

To Hugh, who had last seen the old farm drowsing deserted in the evening sun, the scene which met their eyes as they drove up the elm-lined avenue was a bitter contrast. The fire engine was there and scores of helpers hovered round the house. So far only one side had caught, but the left wing was well and truly blazing. Firemen were turning their hoses on it, trying to keep the flames from spreading.

One glance told him, however, that his fears for the animals had been needless. The shippen and stables were untouched, though the haystack had caught some sparks. He was soon to find that the animals had been let out and turned into the fields as soon as the alarm was given.

J. B. stopped at the top of the drive. A man, whom he seemed to know, ran forward. "All right, sir, they're getting it under control," he shouted. "Luckily there's plenty of water."

Clover remained in the car—she could do nothing but hinder, with her injured foot hampering her movements. Tim and Hugh followed Nicky's tall figure across the lawn and were soon indistinguishable among the crowds of helpers. Fortunately the fire-engine was large and up-to-date, but even so willing hands passed pails of water in an unending chain from the pool behind the stables and these were thrown, often with more energy than judgment, into the inferno which was the left wing.

It was a wild scene. Figures showed dark against the flames, and shouts mingled with the lowing of the disturbed cows, the startled whinnying of the horses and the cackle of the geese. Now and then Clover could discern Nicky's figure always foremost among the fire-fighters, helping to save the farm which had been so strangely stolen from him for more than a year.

Four jets were now playing on the roof, and slowly, almost imperceptibly, the flames were abating. A low cheer rose when the firemen stood back for a moment to stare at the blackened walls, then, when flames rose again, they went on working.

Clover was sitting so tensely that her good foot developed pins and needles; she was rubbing it when someone came up to the side of the car.

"It's all right, we're getting it under, little cousin." It was Nicky, his face blackened, his flannels stained with smoke and water.

She could afford to laugh." Not so much the little cousin, Nicky. Don't you know I'm nineteen?"

"So you are! But you were twelve as I remember you, still the serious little worrybones."

"I was never a worrybones."

"Remember that time Hugh fell in that pond over

there? You were as white as a sheet and thought he was drowned. He'd only taken in too much water and too many tadpoles, neat."

Clover began to giggle, and if there was a note of hysteria in the sound it wasn't to be wondered at. Nicky laughed too, then went back to his work.

Another hour found the battle fought and won. Many of the helpers from the village had drifted away, but the firemen remained in case the embers caught again.

Hugh, Nicky and Tim helped to get the animals back to their quarters—no easy task, as they were all frightened and confused by the break in their routine.

Clover was actually feeling sleepy when J. B. walked up and got into the driver's seat.

"Time we got you back," he said, "pity you came really."

"Is it safe to leave it now?"

"Nicky's staying, and a couple of firemen too."

"Oh." Clover was disappointed. If Nicky had returned with them he might have found time to tell them what lay behind his strange return; now she must wait.

When Tim and Hugh appeared, filthy and soaking wet, but cheerful, she lay back feeling useless; she had come and just sat there like a log. Still, it had been better than waiting at home and worrying, sleepless, through the hours.

"The mystery is," said Hugh as he got in next to her, "how the fire broke out. They suspect the vaults, but they're of stone and difficult to ignite."

"It was part of a plan," J. B., who had not yet started

the car, turned, "Smiler had to conceal something, and something big, before he made his getaway."

"To think," wailed Clover, "that he has got away like this after carrying on for nearly a year at goodness knows what!"

J. B. gave her one of his whimsical glances. "And how do you know that he has got away?"

"I say," cried Hugh, "have they caught him? Mr. Smith, you know they have!"

The older man shook his head. "I'm not one to give away official information until it is official, but yes, I think I can say that for once Mr. 'Smiler' Garth has been just a bit too clever." He would say no more, but brother and sister exchanged glances, intercepted by Tim who nodded proudly. His faith in J. B. had been justified, said that nod.

A tall figure waved to them as they turned down the avenue, waved and turned back to the house behind. It was Nicky who had elected to remain and sleep, after eight long years, in his own home again.

"But what happened to him?" murmured Clover sleepily.

Hugh laughed. "Have patience. Surely you've enough to think over to-night, old girl. He'll tell you in his own good time."

J. B. left them at home, then drove away, promising to see them in the morning.

Much to her surprise Clover slept heavily that night. It had been a rather overwhelming day, but at least Bette was safe, she had had J. B.'s word for that and she knew she could trust him.

They were all late next morning. Clover scored by

rising first and had breakfast on the table before the boys were down.

They hurried through the meal and Tim got busy sweeping out the shop and polishing the windows as though nothing had happened. He opened at nine prompt and was already dealing with children buying buckets and spades when J. B. drove up, Nicky with him.

"How's everything at the farm?" was Hugh's first question.

"O.K., might have been very much worse," said Nicky. "I've got in old Selwyn and a son of his to help already. People are being very kind, and curious too. It isn't often they have the chance of meeting two blokes with the same name and the same looks as near as makes no matter. 'I allays knowed there was sumpin rum about that 'un,' old Selwyn told me. 'You'd never 'ave turned me orf, you wouldn't. Stands to reason 'twasn't you.' You see, just plain common sense."

Nicky was now his old self—he teased Clover, laughed at Tim and even made game of the shop, pricing things and insisting on buying a ridiculous monkey carved by Hugh "for a mascot."

J. B. broke in on their laughter and talk. "You people free to leave the shop this morning?"

"What for?" asked Clover, "though of course we can. Tim can easily take charge, he's a better salesman than I am."

"Well," said J. B., "Nicky here is anxious to renew acquaintance with all his cousins so I thought we'd run over and collect Bette."

Clover clasped her hands excitedly. "So you do know

where she is, really and truly? Oh, I knew she was safe if you said so, but I wasn't sure you knew exactly where she was."

Hugh laughed. "The girl's rambling. My word though, do let's go, I'd give something to see the poor kid again."

"All right then, we'll start now."

Clover gave him an inquiring look, then limped off to get her coat. Within a few minutes they were in the car with Tim waving to them from the door, looking pleased, and, as Hugh put it, "like a dog with two tails" at being left in charge.

"Is it far?" asked Clover.

J. B. did not seem to hear—he was making some remark to Nicky, who sat with him.

"Really, Clover, pull yourself together," chaffed Hugh. "You've been positively naïve since they arrived. By the way, notice anything?"

"No. What do you mean?"

"You don't? No policeman about—seems we're no longer under suspicion."

Clover laughed. "You know, I'd forgotten all about that. But he was a nice policeman, I shall always smile when I see him now."

They were driving steadily along the road which passed the farm. As they came to it, they all stared at it in the distance. It looked a little, as Nicky put it ruefully, "dishevelled," the garden trampled on and the left wing a ruin, but the greater part was still standing, cows cropped placidly in the fields, the geese and chickens cackled and clucked in the paddock.

They drove on.

"Where is he taking us?" asked Clover.

"This is the way to Penvale," Hugh told her, "perhaps Bette took refuge somewhere there."

They passed through Penvale though and on towards the forest, and, once the tree-shaded road met them, their driver drove more slowly as though looking for a turning. He found it at last: a lane which was almost a forest ride winding up and down between the bracken and oaks. He drove very slowly now, scanning the trees on the right. It was Clover who saw it first, the roofs of a cottage rising, it seemed, from the forest itself.

"Gosh, of course, I might have known!" cried Hugh. The car stopped before a little wooden gate.

"Where is this?" asked Clover.

"Bracken Cottage. Remember the old lady, Miss Benham?"

Nicky had got out followed by J. B. Hugh and Clover joined them and they stood looking at the neat little place with its steep roofs and latticed windows, and its bright garden full of mid-summer flowers. Then a loud yapping broke the woodland quiet and a small terrier bounded up to the gate.

Nicky opened the gate and the terrier circled round them. A brown spaniel rose from her sunny corner on the lawn and moved, growling deep in her throat, towards them, her three puppies disporting themselves on the grass.

They were moving towards the porch when the owner appeared. She was a little white-haired old lady and Clover easily recognised her from Hugh's description. It was she who had helped Bette after her ordeal in the forest.

Now, calling the dogs, she came forward in quiet

dignity. She smiled at Hugh, whom she recognised, then bowed somewhat coldly to J. B. Smith.

"So you've come again. I think I told you that the dolls would not be ready for another week."

He met her eyes with his bright grey ones.

"You needn't worry, Miss Benham, any time. We want to see your guest, we've got a big surprise for her."

Even as he spoke a slim figure wearing an old fashioned dress of muslin which came down to her feet, came running down the steps to them. It was Bette.

"Clover, Hugh, darlings!" She gave Clover a hug, then stopped, her hands falling to her sides. She was staring at Nicky who stood smiling at her.

"But this is Nicky, the real Nicky! As though I could ever . . ." she broke off, her face flushing, then, as Clover had done, caught his arms as though to make sure he was real.

"Oh Nicky, as though I could ever forget you . . . I'd have known you anywhere . . . why?"

He held her at arm's length.

"Sure it's Nicky, and this is Bette, the little Bette I remember."

She stood still now and her eyes filled with tears.

"I don't understand but I'm so glad!" Suddenly she began to cry in real earnest, cry then laugh with the tears running down her face. It was an extraordinary performance and Clover went to her side.

"Darling, it's all right, that man's gone, they've all gone and Nicky is here safe and well. Don't cry, Bette!"

"I'm not crying," protested Bette, the tears still

running down her cheeks. "I'm laughing!" and she laughed just to prove it.

Old Miss Benham, who had been a confused witness to the little scene interposed gently. "Suppose you all come in. I can only offer you lemonade, I fear, but I did make some cakes yesterday. Yes that's right, do come in. Bette, lead the way. These are your cousins, of course. I have met Hugh as I told you but not the girl. Poor dear, she still has to use a stick, I see."

Once in the old lady's small room they all began to talk at once. Bette, who had regained her composure, handed round glasses of lemonade and cakes: they drank the lemonade, though none of them felt like eating.

"But Bette," began Clover, when she could get a word in, "what happened? We knew you came here, then you disappeared. That man said you had taken the train to London from Penvale, but we soon found out you hadn't."

Bette's vivid face sobered. "I had the rottenest luck. I got a lift and the man in the lorry was one of that man's gang. He took me straight back to the farm and they put me in the vaults."

Hugh stared. "You mean the cellars?"

"Yes, I was there until Sunday, or rather early on Monday morning, then Mrs. Della helped me escape. But I had to promise her that I'd remain hidden until a week had passed or he'd do something awful to her." She stopped.

J. B. Smith looked at her kindly.

"Finish your drink, then. If you like you can tell us now, or wait—it doesn't really matter."

Bette met Clover's eager glance. "I'll tell them now," she said. "I say, who are you? Wasn't it you I ran into in the dark that awful morning in the garden at the farm?"

"Yes, it was I. I was keeping a watch on the place. I've a bone to pick with you, by the way."

Bette blushed. "I say, I know I kicked out really hard. You see I thought you were one of the gang."

J. B. rubbed a shin reminiscently. "I've still got the bruise. Never mind, my dear. Shoot!"

And there in Miss Benham's little room, with the others listening, sometimes interrupting, but always listening, Bette told her story.

CHAPTER TWELVE

WHAT HAPPENED TO BETTE

"I WAS livid with fear," Bette began, "but strangely enough I slept quite heavily that first night in that underground place. I knew that the man who called himself Nicholas Ferndale would be bound to return soon, and I'd practically told him that I knew he wasn't Nicky." She broke off. "Miss Benham told me that Ian Trent had been found and taken to hospital. Who found him?"

"The police," J. B. told her, "they were rung up early on Saturday morning."

Bette's face glowed. "Dear Bobby, I knew he'd do it. Clever boy, he daren't tell his father straight out, so he must have rung up."

"But go on," cried Clover, in an agony of impatience.

Bette clasped her hands, and sat very still, an incongruously old-fashioned figure in the muslin frock which was obviously one of Miss Benham's. Then in a carefully controlled voice she told them about that Friday night, going back to the time when she had traced the message in the dust, rung up from the call-box and her discovery of the injured man in the quarry. She detailed her flight to the forest and its sequel, culminating in her final capture when she had innocently boarded a van on the Penvale road.

She went back to her experiences imprisoned in the vaults and how she had found the concealed door and what lay beyond.

"When I saw the printing press I knew. The man who had taken Nicky's identity was a forger in a big way—he was using the farm as a hideout and his gang were with him."

"Good lord!" cried Nicky.

J. B. nodded. "Yes, the police had been very worried about a flow of excellently made forged notes. At first they thought that they had been smuggled in from the continent, probably by air. It was a chance which led them to him, Ian Trent's crash, and Bette, of course."

"That explains the fire then," said Nicky, "though there are some traces in the left wing to convict him."

"A fire!" cried Bette.

"It's not so bad," said Hugh quickly, "Grange Farm is still standing—the firemen got there in time to save the greater part of it."

Miss Benham wrung her hands. "There now, I thought I saw a glare in the sky last night and in that direction, but I said nothing—the poor child had been worried enough."

"Do go on," pleaded Clover.

Bette smiled round her. "Well, as I told you, when I woke that Sunday morning in that awful underground room I was terrified. I paced about, but to escape was impossible. I could see the green bank beyond the moat through the bars of the grating, but it was impossible to get out that way. When Mrs. Della came in with my breakfast I asked her if the Boss, as she called him, had come back yet. She said he had returned last night and, as she put it, he was in a nasty temper. 'It's a pity you ever saw this place,' she told me, as though I didn't know that already. I asked her why she worked for him and she told me. I suppose she felt it didn't matter what she told me then. Her husband had worked for the Boss and was now in prison. The Boss had promised to help him when he came out and, meanwhile, he'd given her the job of cook-housekeeper. I saw that she was in his power and it didn't seem any good asking her to help me. I asked her to let me know what he planned to do. She seemed sorry for me. 'He'll be down soon. I'd act stupid if I was you,' she said.

"Hours seemed to pass after that, but it was midday when he came in at last. I went cold when the door was unlocked and he strolled in looking calm and collected as though he were paying a morning call. He actually smiled, but the smile didn't reach his eyes, it never does. He didn't seem even angry.

"'You might as well let me go,' I said, 'I'll join my Aunt in Scotland. I won't say anything.'

"He sat on the edge of the camp bed, leaving me standing, and lit a cigarette.

"'You won't say anything about what?' he asked.

"I tried to speak lightly. 'About coming to see you when it wasn't convenient!'

"'A pity you did, a pity too that you are intelligent, and endowed with the usual feminine curiosity.' You know the way he talks—cool and pleasant but steely underneath.

"I asked him to let me go and I'd forget everything." Bette looked at them all apologetically. "You see I was frightened. I knew what he'd done to Ian Trent."

Nicky smiled. "Believe me, Bette, I'd have done the same in your place."

"I don't think you would. Anyhow it wasn't a bit of good. He looked me over then said. 'How very accommodating. Suppose I do let you go and you return to the bosom of your family. You may be quiet at first, then you'll start thinking *I must really tell them. I don't think he should get away with it.* You see I know human nature very well indeed.'

"'What will you do with me then?' I asked. I can see him now staring at the red tip of his cigarette.

"'This place is well hidden, none but a favoured few know of its existence. No one knows you are here. They think you have joined your mother in London.'

"'Is she back?' I cried.

"He shrugged. 'I've no idea. One story seemed as good as another. Clover and Hugh think so. They are the only ones, apart from your own people, that is if you have written to them in so short a time, who know you were here.'

"I don't think I said anything then. He began to tick items off on his fingers. 'Now let me see: you know that Ian Trent didn't go off with a friend, that this dear old place is not what it seems, and, you think that I am not your beloved Nicky.'

"I gave myself away completely then.

"'Who are you?' I asked.

"He stood up. 'There you are, you will ask awkward questions. I think a little more solitary confinement is indicated until I have perfected my plans.' He gave me a long look with those cold pitiless eyes of his and left me. I knew I'd lost and that the hope that he'd let me go had been absurd.

"I don't like to think back on those next hours. I was even more afraid—I'd nothing to do, nothing to read, no lunch came, and when, at five that evening, Mrs. Della came with a jug of cocoa and some sandwiches, I ran forward, glad to have anyone to speak to.

"She put down the tray in a furtive manner, and looked at me in her funny cold way. What she said gave me hope again.

"'If I could trust you,' she said, 'he doesn't, that's sure, you're in his way. But I had a daughter like you once, fair she was.'

"I caught her arm. 'Get me out and I'll do anything for you.'

"'I don't want no rewards,' she said, 'all I ask is that you stay quiet and hidden for one week. Where could you go?'

"I was pretty crazy with relief. 'To my cousins, I could go into Fairham by dark.'

"'Them, no! They'd ask questions and you'd be tempted to tell 'em things.'

"I thought wildly, then I remembered you, Miss Benham. I knew how kind you were, that you'd take me in and that you lived absolutely off the beaten track. I told her about you and she nodded.

"'I think I know the place, a bit of a cottage off the Penvale Road.'

"'That's it.'

"'It's a good seven miles by road, but if you take the lane beyond the quarry and cut round by the forest, 'tis a matter of five.' She stopped then. 'I'll be back later,' she promised, and left me, her face as blank as ever, but what a difference she had made. I just paced about, like those poor caged animals one sees in zoos. A great storm blew up—thunder seemed to echo round the tiny room and the rain began to pelt into the moat. I sat and watched the lightning then got up and paced about again.

"Night came down but it still rained. I flung myself down on the bed. At first I couldn't sleep, but I suppose I must have dozed off for I was wakened by the grinding of the heavy door and it was Mrs. Della again.

"She carried a torch. I sat up and pulled on my shoes She told me it was almost three in the morning. 'I had to wait,' she said. 'Now you'll promise to stay with the old lady? Remember it's my skin and my man's at stake!' I held on to her. I asked her to let me know her address and I'd get Mother to send her something for helping me, but she only shook me off. 'All I want you to do is keep quiet. Now follow me.'

"Well, I followed her up and through the house and

out into the yard. She had put a coat over her head and saw me to the edge of the garden, indicating the road round the quarry which I knew only too well led to the forest. It was pitch dark and still raining but she gave me a torch. Her last words were 'A whole week, mind, and keep your word.'

"I promised and rushed off." Bette stopped and looked pleadingly around her. "I've broken my word now telling you all, but . . ."

J. B. shook his head. "You needn't worry, everything is already known by the police and not through you."

Bette looked at him with the flicker of a smile then continued. "I was rushing towards the road when a man appeared from the trees and caught me by the arms.

He didn't sound like one of the gang. He only said something about what was I doing out so late and he had an educated voice, but I was frantic and thought it might be a friend of that man's so I kicked out hard and he let me go."

She glanced wryly across at J. B. He only smiled, but his eyes were twinkling.

She leaned back and sipped some lemonade.

"That's nearly all. I found my way to the cottage, It seemed an endless walk and it was dawn before I got there. Miss Benham, like the angel she is, took me in again and I'm afraid I didn't tell her much save that I wanted to stay and rest for a while. She must have thought that I made a habit of rambling about in the night, but she fed me and put me to bed, and I told her everything when I was rested and this time she believed me." She put out her hand and caught the old lady's. "Didn't you?"

"Yes, my dear, it's a wicked world, it really is. I never heard of such wickedness."

"We had a visitor yesterday," went on Bette, a mischievous tone in her voice, "but he didn't seem to suspect anything."

J. B. laughed outright. "When charming old ladies like Miss Benham here receive harmless strangers suspiciously, it is always the sign of a guilty conscience. And I did glimpse you as you slipped away through the garden, and very glad I was to do so. I knew that you were still safe."

"Did you follow me that night?" asked Bette.

"After I had recovered from a bruised shin, I certainly did. Not difficult in the rain and you were pickng your way with the torch. Anyhow I knew you were all right, or when the farm was on fire I should have had some very nasty moments."

Bette whitened. "Do you mean it was on fire where I was imprisoned?"

"The fire, my dear, started in the vaults."

Nicky sprang to his feet. "The scoundrel! Even after what he did to me I didn't think he'd contemplate a thing like that."

"He didn't," J. B. told him, "he fired the farm to destroy traces of the forging plant, but he made sure that Bette was out of the way first. At least he had that decency."

Bette stared. "You mean that he knew Mrs. Della set me free?"

"I'm sure of it. She was primed with the story she told you. He judged that you would stay quiet in your refuge here for her sake. As he told you, he knew human nature and enough about you to judge that you wouldn't let down a woman who had trusted you."

"What a strange man he is," said Bette. She looked at Nicky. "But you, Nicky, where have you been all this time?"

They all stared at the young man who had sat grimly listening to his young cousin's story.

He grinned. "All right, here goes. The man whom you knew as Nicholas Ferndale, who took my identity, is called, as far as we know, Evan Garth, known to his familiars as 'Smiler'. He was in Cyprus mixed up with some bandits and I found him with them when I was wounded, captured and taken to the hills. In figure, general appearance and colouring, he was very like me, as you know. We seemed to be both in the same fix at the mercy of those rascals and we got talking and became quite friendly. Now, of course, I realise how he pumped me about my home life. I became ill with dysentry before we were released and he took the trouble to look me up in the hospital and suggested that as soon as I was well and got leave that I came for a cruise in the Mediterranean in his little yacht. I gathered that he had not been in the army but involved in Cyprus during one of the many troubles there and was apparently a rich man. When I got the necessary leave I accepted—frankly I rather liked the chap and was still feeling pretty dicky. Anyhow it was only a matter of time before I left the army, and, as my father had died and the farm was prospering with Hugh and Clover in charge, I saw no reason why I shouldn't take this unexpected holiday for a short while. He had suggested a fortnight." He turned to Clover and Hugh. "I wrote to you telling you all about it, didn't you get my letter?"

"No," said Hugh, "not a word. Only the letter when you were in hospital, but now I remember you did say you were thinking of taking a cruise."

Nicky nodded. "As I thought. I gave the letter to one of Smiler's men to post. Well, the yacht was surprisingly big. Later I found that Smiler was in league with a Levantine merchant of dubious reputation and she was his. She was manned by the toughest lot of men I've ever seen, yellow, black or white. We sailed round the Isles of Greece, stopped and went up to Athens and I enjoyed it very much. I played cards with Smiler and we talked. He is an interesting fellow, with funds of good stories. Then one night, a choppy night when we were a few score knots from Greece, I was assaulted, knocked on the head and thrown overboard." He paused.

They all stared at him appalled.

"How absolutely foul!" exclaimed Hugh.

"I agree. Smiler had no scruples. He wanted to return to England and he was getting short of money. My place, a farm in working order and isolated, was just what he wanted. However, it just so happened that I was lucky. I told you it was a choppy night and the wind had driven us off our course. I was picked up by some Greek fishermen who took me to land and cared for me. But when I came to myself I was faced with a complete blackout. I couldn't remember a thing, my papers which showed my identity, army papers, money, everything, had been taken from me; for a time I was a man without a memory or an identity. An English doctor was called and I was sent up to hospital in Athens and there I stayed. For six months I lived in a no man's land, then gradually my memory returned. I talked with the authorities, got in touch with the British Consul and must have given them all several headaches for it was soon discovered that Nicholas Ferndale had long ago been drafted back to England and been demobbed. He was now, I was told, settled in his own home. Well, back I came to England and arrived home, a human question mark: no name and no papers to prove my name. I was kept under observation for a time, then," he smiled at J. B., "you turned up this week and I was allowed to come up here and make my own discoveries."

Bette stared at J. B. in incredulity.

"But, Mr. Smith, how did you come into all this? How did you find out about Nicky?"

Nicky agreed: "That's what's puzzling me."

J. B. asked permission of Miss Benham, who sat looking more and more bewildered, then lit a pipe.

"Until last week I was in the South of France with my wife. I was called back to consult with Scotland Yard about the increasing forged notes being found. Then private reasons also brought me, by an odd coincidence, to this part of the country. I'll go into those later. Well, I visited Grange Farm. The owner did not know me, but I knew him in spite of the beard. He had been in a very nasty gang just after the war, a gang which specialised in forgery and worse; he'd come up against the law then, but got away and on to the Continent. He was no more Ferndale than I was, and I knew that the odd telephone message passed on to me about the missing pilot had something to do with him. I returned to London and inquiries soon put me on to the nameless man who stated that he was the real Nicholas. The rest you know. I saw you, Nicky, and advised you to come up here. Too late; Smiler had made his escape and all was over but the shouting."

There was a short silence; the two stories had been so amazing that comment was unnecessary.

Miss Benham stood up. "I think Bette ought to rest now, she's looking very pale."

Bette caught her hand. "You can see what I've had to put up with since I came here—talk about spoiling!"

J. B. stood up too. "I must return to town to-day sometime and we mustn't encroach on Miss Benham like this. Nicky, I suppose you're staying at the farm?"

"Of course, there's lots to be done. I've got to rally up my old workers, those I can get hold of."

J. B. smiled at Hugh and Clover. "And you to your business?" He looked at Bette consideringly. "Now Bette, no need for you to remain in hiding any longer. Shall I run you up to London?"

"I'll go back with Hugh and Clover, if they'll have me."

He looked at her, head on one side. Bette had the impression that he, J. B., was slightly embarrassed.

"I happen to know that your mother is back in London."

"But how . . . she'll have got my letter, of course. I do hope she hasn't been worried," said Bette.

"A little, I'm afraid. But I've been able to calm her fears." Bette stared at J. B. and J. B. met her stare, smiling.

"Well, I'd love to join her of course but . . . Clover, I'll have to come back and get my other case."

"Good. Then why not say good-bye to Miss Benham

for the present and I'll drive you to Town. We can stop on the way for you to get your clothes."

"It's kind of you, but oughtn't I to wire Mummy first?"

"I've already rung her up, she will be expecting you. She doesn't know the whole story yet, so when we do get there, let her down gently or I shall get into trouble." He broke off, "I hope you'll like your room—we've both taken some pains with it."

"Do you know Mummy well, then?"

Again J. B. looked almost embarrassed. He lit another match for his pipe and said, "I ought to have told you before, I suppose, but I thought you might have guessed. Still, Smith is such a common name..." he seemed to pull himself together and went on: "I'm J. Barton Smith, but everyone calls me J. B. When your mother got your letter saying you were with Nicholas, she was worried, but not so worried as I was. I was almost certain by that time that he was an impostor. So that's why I just came down here."

Bette digested this in silence and it was Clover who gave a little exclamation.

"So you're the wicked step-father!"

"*You* are?" murmured Bette.

He bowed. "At your service, and very sorry I am that it has been such a queer introduction. Anyway, how do you do, Bette, I hope we shall be friends."

Bette reddened. This was the man she had almost hated in thought and resented. Why, she actually liked him!

"I'm sure we shall," she said tamely.

He put his hand on her shoulder and gave her a little squeeze.

"Won't be my fault if we don't," he said kindly.

As they all packed into the car and waved to Miss Benham standing with her animals at the gate, Clover remarked in undertones to her brother that she hoped that the day was finished with surprise. "I don't think I could bear any more."

"He's a decent sort," murmured Hugh, "Bette's taken to him already."

"And won't Tim be thrilled when he knows that the great J. B. is one of the family," added Clover.

They had almost forgotten Tim, but he was there in the shop with the news that he had made various sales, looking very important and pleased with himself.

"So Bette's O.K.," he remarked as, after a quick word with him, Bette hurried with Clover to find her case and change out of her rather outlandish dress.

Hugh nodded. "We've heard everything now, Tim. Do you know that . . . ?"

The shop bell went. Tim put up his hand. "Just a minute, I'll hear all later, I've a customer," he said.

For with Tim Benson, business came first.

Grange Farm stood, its doors wide to the air and sun. All was quiet, for the builders who had almost completed the repairs on the gutted left wing had long since gone.

However the lawn was not deserted; two people sat there in garden chairs: a fair, pretty woman with Bette's clear grey eyes, and a broad genial-looking man who watched her pour out tea as he put away the inevitable pipe.

"Clover and Hugh are late," remarked Mrs. Smith. "Don't eat up all the scones, John, before they come."

He grinned. "I shall unless they hurry. Anyhow here comes my daughter and the long lost heir."

Bette and Nicky were coming down the slope beyond the garden. Bette, her fair hair shining, looked full of life and fun. She had gathered an armful of foxgloves, and Nicky was teasing her.

"As though we haven't enough flowers in the garden, you must tear up those wild things."

"I picked them very carefully. I just had to peep in at the forest. It's lovely really—to-day," she added, her face clouding.

"Now, no looking back! You promised!"

Bette nodded. "I have fogotten the bad parts—almost. I try and think of it as just an exciting adventure. Fancy that man in prison, Nicky!"

"Yes, thanks to J. B. they caught him just in time. He was making for the Continent in a private plane."

"And my stepfather guessed what he'd do and got in touch with the R.A.F. who helped get him down," finished Bette, and she sounded proud to say "stepfather", as she was.

"Forget it. Here come Clover and Hugh in their old claptrap. Tim persuaded them that that car was a bargain for fifty pounds—at least it goes."

"And he's with them," cried Bette, "he must have got back from London." They hurried down just in time to meet the three newcomers getting out of the pre-war Austin.

"Look who's here," said Clover. "Nicky, he's made up his mind he's going to manage the shop for me whilst I go to sales. We've even found him a room just down Fore Street and he starts on Monday."

Tim was one big smile. "Suits me. I worked on Mum, told her the doctor always said I needed a country life away from the racket of Fleet Street. I bet I'll double the sales in a year. By the way," he said to Hugh, "we could do with some more of those toys of yours—you're neglecting them since you turned farmer."

Hugh laughed. "Come the long winter nights I'll turn them off by the score, but this is our busiest time."

Clover gave him a proud look. Only she knew how he had felt when he had had to give up the farm and take a job in an office. The return of the real Nicky had changed all that. He had taken his young cousin as a partner and, as Hugh was a born farmer, both had benefited.

Bette's mother was waving to them.

"Come along, all of you, tea's getting cold and John's started on the cakes!"

Bette hurried forward. Her mother looked younger and happier and J. B. was all a step-father should be, humorous, kind and never, never patronising.

Certainly she had not yet got over the fact that John Barton Smith, whom her mother had married, was the famous crime lawyer who worked for a national newspaper and was often called in by Scotland Yard. Indeed, when she remembered those terrible days a month ago, she did not know what would have happened had not her mother become uneasy and her step-father decided to investigate.

Old Mrs. Jennings, a stout and homely body who had been reinstated as Nicky's housekeeper on his return, brought out more tea; they found chairs and sat in a little circle round the garden table. They had settled themselves when J. B. remarked:

"Hugh, we'll need another chair."

"Why, isn't the party complete?" cried Bette, "we were only expecting Clover and Hugh, Tim gate-crashed anyhow."

"There is someone who happens to be staying in the neighbourhood and promised to drop in." J. B.'s eyes held a twinkle as he spoke. His wife poured out more tea.

"What have you been up to now, John?"

He would say no more but the twinkle lingered. In fact they were all talking and laughing and did not hear the sound of a car in the avenue until it reached the drive.

It was an old sports car, shabby but powerful, and out of it got a figure in Air Force blue.

Bette stared. "No! It can't be!"

Her step-father smiled. "Yes, someone's come to renew acquaintance with you and Grange Farm."

The tall figure, which moved quickly across the garden towards them, was at least familiar to Bette.

"Hallo, everybody, hallo J. B.!" Ian Trent smiled round him, then his eyes fell on Bette who flushed.

Introductions followed and he flung himself on the grass next to Bette's chair.

"I say, it's good to see you again. You got my letter?"

"Yes, and thank you."

"For expressing a little appreciation? You saved my life, didn't you?"

She looked at the brown face and met the blue eyes which, when she had last seen them, had been so full of distress. For she had not seen him since he had left hospital. It was just like J. B. to spring this surprise on them.

Bette's mother was looking at him with interest.

"It was you who started all the queer business around here, wasn't it?" she said.

"Yes, when I crashed on the hillside, things started humming. Perhaps as well in a way."

"Poor Bette had a dreadful time," said her mother with a shudder.

"I know, and acted like a little Trojan. You should be proud of your daughter, Mrs. Smith."

She smiled, for she was.

It was Tim who, during a short silence which can fall on the gayest crowd, said in his eager voice:

"I say, about that box. Were all those notes duds—I mean forgeries?"

J. B. shook his head. "No they were real notes, save for one or two, but the plates were enough to convict the owner. Your friend Smiler left them with you—in safe keeping as he thought—he must have had a very bad moment when the Inspector was there."

"And put the can on Hugh and Clover," added Tim.

"What is all this?" asked the young airman.

They told him about the box consigned to Clover, and the conversation inevitably returned to those sinister days when Bette had been missing and Ian himself ill and unconscious in hospital.

He glanced at Bette.

"I'll say you've had your fill of adventure and mystery."

Bette agreed vehemently. "I never want to get involved in another mystery or take part in another adventure again, not even in book form," she added.

Her step-father gave her an indulgent smile.

"And what was the name of the book I saw you poring over late last night when you should have been in bed?" he asked.

Bette made a little face at him and everybody laughed.

And so it was that the sinister incidents at Grange Farm ended for them all, in laughter and a new feeling of security.